Loretta's hand clasped her midsection, her eyes wide.

Panic whipped through Griffin. "Are you having the baby?"

Shaking her head, Loretta took Griffin's hand and planted it on her swollen belly. "She—or he—just kicked me. Here, feel."

The heat of her body scorched his hand. He wanted to pull back, but she held him there. And then the baby kicked.

To actually feel the movement, to imagine a tiny foot pressing against his hand, touched him in a way he certainly hadn't expected. An odd lump formed in his throat. He gazed into Loretta's liquid-brown eyes, and they wouldn't let him go. At some gut level, Griffin wanted to pledge he'd be there to take care of this baby, but he couldn't do that. He wasn't a family man.

With a force of will, he broke the connection between them and stepped back. He was not going to get involved with this woman or her baby.

Except that he already was....

Dear Reader,

The end of the century is near, and we're all eagerly anticipating the wonders to come. But no matter what happens, I believe that everyone will continue to need and to seek the unquenchable spirit of love…of *romance*. And here at Silhouette Romance, we're delighted to present another month's worth of terrific, emotional stories.

This month, RITA Award-winning author Marie Ferrarella offers a tender BUNDLES OF JOY tale, in which *The Baby Beneath the Mistletoe* brings together a man who's lost his faith and a woman who challenges him to take a chance at love…and family. In Charlotte Maclay's charming new novel, a millionaire playboy isn't sure what he was *Expecting at Christmas,* but what he gets is a *very* pregnant butler! Elizabeth Harbison launches her wonderful new theme-based miniseries, CINDERELLA BRIDES, with the fairy-tale romance—complete with mistaken identity!—between *Emma and the Earl*.

In *A Diamond for Kate* by Moyra Tarling, discover whether a doctor makes his devoted nurse his devoted wife *after* learning about her past…. Patricia Thayer's cross-line miniseries WITH THESE RINGS returns to Romance and poses the question: Can *The Man, the Ring, the Wedding* end a fifty-year-old curse? You'll have to read this dramatic story to find out! And though *The Millionaire's Proposition* involves making a baby in Natalie Patrick's upbeat Romance, can a down-on-her-luck waitress also convince him to make beautiful memories…as man and wife?

Enjoy this month's offerings, and look forward to a new century of timeless, traditional tales guaranteed to touch your heart!

Mary-Theresa Hussey

Mary-Theresa Hussey
Senior Editor, Silhouette Romance

Please address questions and book requests to:
Silhouette Reader Service
U.S.: 3010 Walden Ave., P.O. Box 1325, Buffalo, NY 14269
Canadian: P.O. Box 609, Fort Erie, Ont. L2A 5X3

EXPECTING AT CHRISTMAS

Charlotte Maclay

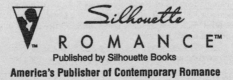

Silhouette
R O M A N C E™
Published by Silhouette Books
America's Publisher of Contemporary Romance

For my great-nephew—wear your name proudly!

SILHOUETTE BOOKS

ISBN 0-373-19409-9

EXPECTING AT CHRISTMAS

Visit us at www.romance.net

Printed in U.S.A.

Books by Charlotte Maclay

Silhouette Romance

Only Bachelors Need Apply #1249
Expecting at Christmas #1409

Books by Charlotte Maclay writing as Charlotte Moore

Silhouette Romance

Not the Marrying Kind #975
Belated Bride #1088
The Maverick Takes a Wife #1129

Silhouette Shadows

Trust Me #62

CHARLOTTE MACLAY

has always enjoyed putting words on paper. Until recently, most of these words have been nonfiction, including a weekly newspaper column, which has recruited nearly twenty thousand volunteers in the past twenty years for some four hundred different local non-profit organizations.

When she is not urging people to get involved in their community, Charlotte divides her time among writing, volunteering for her favorite organizations (including Orange County Chapter of Romance Writers of America), trying *not* to mother two married daughters and sharing her life in Southern California with her own special hero, Chuck.

Dear Santa,

It's been a long time since I've written a list to you, but this year, maybe because the baby will be here soon and it will be his or her first Christmas, there are a few things I would wish for to make this holiday just perfect.

1) For my brother Roberto, a new tow truck for his business

2) My brother Marco could sure use some new pizza pans to replace the banged-up ones he uses at his restaurant

3) Nothing pleases dear Aunt Louisa more than skeins of tatting yarn, so I'd wish for a basket of yarn for her that magically would never get empty

4) Now I know my cousin Brenna would love a mini second honeymoon with her husband….

5) And as for me, I don't want much for Christmas—but with all my heart I wish for a healthy baby with ten fingers, ten toes and an adorable smile. That would do me just fine.

Of course, if I were being totally honest, I'd want a daddy for my baby—and a husband for me. But I don't suppose I'd ever find one in your pack. Still, there's no harm in asking….

Merry Christmas.

Love,

Loretta Santana

Chapter One

Getting a job was always difficult. Landing one when you were eight months pregnant counted as a miracle.

Loretta Santana smoothed her hair back as she heard her new employer's car cross the narrow wooden bridge at the bottom of Topanga Canyon Road and navigate the circular drive in front of his house.

She'd never actually been a butler before, though she'd taken an accelerated class at the Westside Butler Academy just last week in order to qualify for this position. And, true, her black suit, which she wore with a neat little bow tie, might have been a bit odd to order in a maternity size. But she was determined she'd keep this job until she became eligible for insurance benefits with the temporary agency that had hired her. She only needed one hundred and twenty more hours to her credit—three weeks—and she could sign up. Her baby wasn't due for another four weeks and one day, the week after Christmas.

Instinctively she slid her hand across her distended belly. Both she and Isabella's baby would need the medical benefits.

Anxiety had her gnawing at her lower lip as she opened the front door, standing back so Griffin Jones wouldn't get a full-length look at her right off. Her nerves were certainly frazzled. When she got past this hurdle, she'd have to take a megadose of vitamin E to stabilize her ions and get her yin and yang back in balance.

With the easy strides of an athlete, Griffin mounted the steps two at a time. His suit jacket hung open and his power tie was loose around his collar. He came to an abrupt halt at the front door.

"Well, well, well," he drawled. A wicked smile curled amazingly sensual lips. "What have we got here?"

"Loretta Santana, sir. Your temporary butler."

He glanced past her into the rustic entry with its warm wood paneling and subdued lighting. "What did you do with Rodgers, sweetheart?"

"I believe he's en route to London, sir."

"Oh, I forgot that he had some sort of a family crisis back home." Frowning, he cocked his head to the right, causing a lock of tobacco-brown hair to slide across his forehead at a rakish angle. "And you're somebody's idea of a joke butler?"

She flushed. "No, sir. I'm fully qualified to—"

"I'll just bet you are." He stepped across the threshold, his gaze raking over her with swift, masculine interest until it landed right smack on her midsection. "My God, you're pregnant!" He choked and began coughing.

"Oh, you poor thing. You must have a terrible cold." Automatically she placed the back of her hand to his forehead. "A fever, too. You'd better come inside. I'll brew you a nice herbal toddy and give you some of my rejuvenative hydration pills. You'll be right as rain in no time, sir." Hooking her arm through his, Loretta tried to hustle him toward the master bedroom where he could get the rest he obviously needed—and forget he had a pregnant butler working for him. "Winter colds can be so dreadful. Would you like me to draw a nice hot bath for you, sir? Or can you manage for yourself?"

He put on the brakes. "I don't have a cold, just a little sore throat, and I don't appreciate my buddies playing a practical joke on me. They know damn well I wouldn't sleep with a pregnant woman."

Shock drove her back against the nearest wall. "*Sleep?* I wouldn't— That's not why— The agency wouldn't—" Good grief, what had she gotten herself into?

"That's what this is all about, isn't it? Ol' Brainerd set you up, didn't he? Thought it would be funny to—"

"The employment agency sent me. I needed the job. They didn't say you'd try to *ravish* me."

"I'm not going to do any such—"

Without waiting for his explanation, she made a dash for the kitchen and the connecting servants' quarters. She'd lock herself in, call the police—

"Wait! What the hell—"

She didn't stop. But given her portly figure, her fastest run was more like a slow waddle. He caught up with her at the butcher-block island counter in the kitchen and snared her by the arm.

"Don't hurt the baby. Please don't—"

"For God's sake, I'm not going to hurt you. I just want to know what's going on."

Her chin trembled. He was a really big man, his shoulders broad beneath his suit jacket, and his penetrating eyes so light a shade of blue they flashed like swords of silver. Loretta would not want to sit across a negotiating table from Griffin Jones. He would intimidate the staunchest foe.

She wasn't feeling very staunch at the moment.

"Look, don't cry," he pleaded, loosening his grip on her arm. "I can't stand a weepy woman."

"I'm not weepy." She sniffed.

"Are you saying the employment agency sent you?"

She nodded.

"You sure you didn't just happen to see the article in *Inside Business* about me being one of the ten top eligible bachelors, and you thought you'd claim I was your baby's father—"

"I'd never do such a thing," she gasped. "Isabella never would have wanted to have your baby."

He blinked. "Who's Isabella? I thought your name was Lor—"

"She's my aunt, or she was. My mother's youngest sister. I'm having her baby."

With a shake of his head, Griffin stepped back. Maybe he did have a fever, after all. This woman wasn't making any sense. "Where's your husband?"

"I don't exactly have a husband."

"Okay, then, your boyfriend."

"I don't exactly have one of those, either, not since I got pregnant."

"You figured you'd get pregnant and your boyfriend would have to marry you, huh?" A woman had tried to do that to Griffin not so long ago. He'd been willing to do the right thing. He'd had to. The death of Griffin's mother in childbirth had always haunted him. He'd been nagging his parents for a baby brother, and when it turned out she was pregnant with a girl, he hadn't wanted her. Then, suddenly, his mother was gone and so was his sister. He'd felt guilty ever since and somehow responsible.

And so years later he'd naturally felt responsible for the woman he'd slept with, Amanda Cook—until he discovered she wasn't pregnant at all. She was nothing more than a gold digger anxious to get her hands on the substantial fortune he'd earned running one of the biggest chains of electronic stores in the country. He wouldn't fall for a trick like that again anytime soon; he'd sworn off relationships that even hinted at commitment.

"Oh, no, this isn't Rudy's baby. It's Wayne's."

Wayne? She definitely had an active love life, more than Griffin had managed lately. "So why didn't he marry you?"

"He was married to Isabella."

Now he could see exactly what had happened. "So Isabella caught you playing around with her husband."

"No, of course not." She looked honestly offended he'd suggested that possibility. "I wouldn't do a thing like that. I loved Wayne just like he was my blood uncle."

"And that's why you're having his kid?" Griffin had definitely lost the drift here somewhere.

"Well, Isabella couldn't do it. Somebody had to help them out. So I said I would. Rudy didn't like that. He said it made me 'used goods,' just because I was having their baby." Her chin began to tremble again and her doe eyes started to fill with tears. "That wasn't a very nice thing for him to say, was it?"

Griffin wasn't sure.

"And that's why I really, really need this job, Mr. Jones. But there's no way I'm going to go to bed with you, so you can just forget *that* idea right now."

"It wasn't *my* idea. I thought—" Ah, hell, he didn't know what he'd been thinking. "Look, why don't we just sit down and talk a minute. We can

start from the beginning, have a nice cup of coffee—''

''Herbal tea would be much better for your cold.''

''I don't have a cold.''

''Of course you do. Everybody gets colds during
the winter, especially during the holiday season. It's
nothing to be ashamed of. But I can get your ions
back in shape in no time at all, if you'll just give
me the chance.''

How could a man argue with a woman whose
eyes reminded him of hot chocolate? Particularly a
pregnant woman. ''Okay, we'll do tea and you'll tell
me all about Isabella and Rudy—''

''I don't want to talk about Rudy anymore. I
wouldn't marry him now even if he begged me.''

She scurried to the opposite side of the counter,
opened a cupboard and pulled out a can of what
Griffin assumed was her magical herbal tea. He
hoped he'd be able to gag it down. He suspected
Loretta Santana would get that bruised look in her
dark eyes if he didn't drink every last drop. To his
everlasting dismay, he'd always been a sucker for a
woman with tears in her eyes. Someday he'd learn
his lesson.

''So you can start with Wayne and Isabella,'' he
suggested.

With surprising efficiency, she whipped out a tea-
kettle, filled it with water and placed it on the stove,
then retrieved cups and saucers from another cupboard. She wasn't a large woman, Griffin realized,
maybe five foot two. Her features were delicate, her

cheeks beautifully sculpted. He'd heard pregnant women took on a special glow. With Loretta, he could believe that. Oddly, he didn't want to think about the process that had gotten her pregnant or the man who'd had the privilege. Or the risks a small woman ran by carrying a baby, those same risks that had killed his mother.

"I made you a chicken casserole, if you're hungry. Rodgers wasn't sure you'd be home for dinner."

"You talked to Rodgers?"

"He gave me a full orientation. What time you get up in the mornings, what you like for breakfast—"

"Did he know you were a woman?"

She glanced over her shoulder. "I think he probably noticed."

He grimaced. *Dumb question, Jonesy. You're usually a little smoother with the ladies.* "I just thought it was strange Rodgers would agree to hire a woman as his replacement."

"I told him I could type."

Griffin hoped she'd get the tea ready in a hurry. Maybe it would clear his head. "Why would Rodgers care whether or not you can type?"

Turning, she planted her fists where her waist used to be. "He made it very clear he was not only your butler but also your personal secretary, screening phone calls, keeping your appointment schedule, that sort of thing. I assured him I was quite capable of handling secretarial chores of that very minor sort.''

Choking, Griffin began to cough again. As a part of his job, Rodgers made sure Griffin wasn't interrupted when he was entertaining a lady, keeping phone calls and unexpected guests at bay, particularly when they were other women.

''Oh, my sakes, that cold of yours is just awful. I think I'd better whip up some chicken soup. You know, there's nothing better—''

''No,'' he croaked.

''Really, Mr. Jones, I think—''

''Sit down!'' he bellowed.

She crumpled into the nearest chair at the oak breakfast table, her eyes as wide as flying saucers.

''I'm not going to hurt you,'' he said.

She nodded vigorously, like one of those dolls you see in the back window of souped-up cars.

''I'm just going to explain to you why this isn't going to work, you being my butler and all. It's not personal, you understand. It's that you're a woman.'' *And pregnant.*

Trying to gather himself, Griffin shoved his hands in his pants pockets. His jacket sleeves bunched up and he decided to get rid of the coat, shrugging it off. He took a deep breath. ''Miss Santana, there are various occasions when I have young ladies visiting me. Attractive young ladies. Ladies with whom I sometimes have an intimate relationship.''

A rosy glow crept up her slender neck and stained

her dramatically sculpted cheeks. "I'm not one to judge other people's actions, Mr. Jones."

"Yes, well—" he cleared his throat "—these young ladies, if and when they do visit, might not take kindly to me having a lovely young woman like yourself in my, er, employ." Particularly a sexy, *pregnant* woman, he suspected. And *he* most assuredly didn't like the idea. He didn't want to be *responsible*. What if she fell...or went into early labor? A thousand things could go wrong.

"I wouldn't think of interfering in your personal life, Mr. Jones. They'd never even see me, if that's what you wanted. I'd be still as a mouse." The color on her cheeks went from rose to scarlet, and she raised her chin to a stubborn angle. "Besides, you can't discriminate against me because I'm a woman. The government doesn't allow that anymore. A woman has certain recourses now."

He frowned. He'd had a long day, the competition was gaining the upper hand, and now he had some pregnant woman issuing a veiled threat that she would sue. He didn't like that one damn bit!

"Furthermore, if you're considering discriminating because I happen to be pregnant, you should know forty-two out of the fifty states have laws that prevent discrimination solely for that reason. California is included in that list."

It took him a moment to realize the shrill whistle in his head was the kettle boiling. Scowling, he gestured for her to get the tea.

She hopped up out of her chair like she'd been

goosed. At the counter, she fussed with a teapot and bags of herbal tea while Griffin considered his options. Physically throwing Loretta Santana out of the house wasn't one of them, though he might wish it were. But he just couldn't do that to a pregnant woman—or any other woman, for that matter.

Damn, why had Rodgers's aging mother decided to take a turn for the worse now? She'd been teetering on the edge of whatever for as long as Griffin could remember.

The only reason Griffin had a butler at all was because Rodgers had been with Griffin's father since forever. When his dad died a couple of years ago, Griffin inherited the butler along with a multimillion-dollar company. Bequests like that weren't something a man could turn down.

Loretta slid a cup and saucer onto the table near him. To his amazement it smelled pretty good—a combination of a pine forest and the scent of roses in spring. He sat down and took a sip. He didn't think it would kill him, and maybe it might do something about the raspy throat that had been niggling at him all day.

"So tell me why you want to be my butler."

She eased back into the chair opposite him. In a world of waifs, she'd be a winner. Fragile. Vulnerable. Yet something about the way she held her head suggested a stubborn streak a man would be wise not to challenge.

"It was the only job the agency would send me out on." Her slender shoulders lifted in a shrug.

"Butlers are hard to find nowadays. The pay's not especially good, you know. And I really needed the job so I could get medical coverage for myself and Isabella's baby."

His gaze slid toward her midsection, now hidden by the edge of the table. "You're having somebody else's kid?"

"My aunt tried for years to get pregnant. When she turned forty, she got desperate. They decided to try a surrogate, and I volunteered."

Ah, Isabella and Wayne. The herbal tea was definitely clearing his muddled brain. "You didn't, ah, get that way—" he eyed her hidden belly again "—in the usual way?"

"Oh, my, no. That's an awful thing to even *think* about Uncle Wayne."

"There wasn't anyone else who could do the job? I mean, as a surrogate."

"My other aunts are mostly too old, and my cousins already have children, and their husbands weren't keen on the idea. Besides, most of them didn't have really easy pregnancies."

He clenched a little. Maybe difficult pregnancies ran in her family—high-risk pregnancies. "Couldn't Wayne hire somebody? It couldn't cost much more than—"

"We're family, Mr. Jones. When family's involved, you do what needs to be done."

"I wouldn't give my uncle the time of day, much less get pregnant for him," Griffin grumbled. Besides, Uncle Matt was the competition, the head of the electronic outlet stores that were giving his company fits.

A lyrical giggle erupted from Loretta. "I don't think your uncle is likely to ask you to get pregnant."

"Probably not," he agreed, smiling wryly. He also couldn't imagine his aunt, who looked as dry as a mesquite bush, asking him to impregnate her. He shuddered at the thought. "So why do you need medical insurance? I'd think your aunt and uncle would pay your expenses."

"They died in a car accident."

"I'm sorry. But didn't they leave you something—"

"They weren't rich, Mr. Jones. Not like you. And they never even thought about a will, I'm sure. Even if they had, there wasn't enough left after the double funeral for my medical bills...or the baby's."

God, how he hated sob stories, particularly when they sounded legitimate. "Haven't you been seeing a doctor?"

"Oh, sure. They prepaid my prenatal care, and the doctor's been really good about not charging me for anything extra. But the delivery's a whole different ball game, plus the hospital and pediatric care. So I'm going to need medical insurance." Her eyes started to sparkle again, like diamonds in a pool of hot chocolate.

"Even if I let you work for me until you qualify—and I'm not saying I will," he hastily added when he saw hope spring into her eyes, "wouldn't the insurance company say you've got a pre-existing condition? They won't cover—''

''It works a little differently with temp agencies. If I last long enough, I'm covered since the day I started work for them. It's a carrot they hold out to keep employees around longer.''

''You've worked for these people before, then?''

Nodding, she sipped her tea. ''Lots of times. I work when I'm not going to college.''

''College?''

She lifted her chin again at that determined angle. At some point the dark hair she'd pulled back into a bun had come loose, and feathery strands kissed the slender column of her neck. ''I'm going to be the first person in my whole family who's ever graduated from a university. I've completed 136 units at Cal State L.A.''

''That's a lot of units.'' More than Griffin had, and he had a degree.

''I would have graduated already but I keep changing my major. And they keep changing the requirements.''

''That can set you back, all right.''

''So I've still got a year or so to go. And now with the baby—'' she shrugged ''—it may take me a little longer.''

Maybe she should have thought about that before she agreed to have some other woman's baby. Griffin didn't want anything to do with Loretta and her sob story. He certainly didn't want her as his butler.

But he couldn't exactly throw her out on her ear in the middle of the night.

"Look, Miss Santana—"

"You can call me Loretta, if you like. They said in my accelerated butler's class that was okay, if my employer found it easier."

"Yeah, well…" Damn, he really hated firing people even when they were incompetent. So far, at least, Loretta hadn't done anything wrong. "The truth is, I don't actually need a butler."

"Of course you do. Rodgers assured me—in confidence, you understand—that there are days when you wouldn't be able to manage without him. You're not terribly well organized, I gather."

Griffin scowled. "Rodgers said that?"

"Oh, yes. But you mustn't worry that I'll let you down. I'm the most organized person I know." She appeared quite confident.

He wasn't convinced. "I still don't think—"

The doorbell rang.

"I'll get it." Loretta hopped up, bumping the table in the process with her oversize belly and tipping over her cup of tea. "Oh, dear, I'll wipe that up in a minute. You leave it for me."

"Why don't I answer the door while you take care of—"

"No, no. Answering the door is my job. They taught me just what to do."

Taught her to answer a door? If that's what she learned in the accelerated class, Griffin could barely imagine what a slow course might include.

He heard the door open and Loretta greet his visitor.

"I'm truly sorry you didn't call first, miss," Loretta said. "Mr. Jones has a dreadful cold, and I don't think it would be wise for him to have guests this evening."

A feminine voice he couldn't quite make out responded.

"Now, wait a minute," he muttered, heading for the front of the house. His cold, such as it was, wasn't *that* bad.

"I'm sure you understand Mr. Jones is only thinking of your well-being. He wouldn't want to expose you to a virus that might take weeks for your immune system to throw off."

Griffin spotted a willowy redhead at the door, a soap opera starlet who was making a big splash on the social scene. He'd been trying for weeks to date her.

"Aileen, hi, there. It's good to see you. Come on in." He tried to ease Loretta aside. She didn't budge from her post at the door.

Aileen eyed him with regal disdain before sending Loretta a cutting look intended to cause a mere mortal to bleed profusely. "I don't recall ever getting such an interesting brush-off before, Griffin."

"No, you don't understand. She's my butler."

"Really? How terribly convenient for you." Turning, she floated back down the steps, gracefully exiting the scene.

Griffin swore under his breath and followed her to her flashy Porsche. He tried to talk to Aileen, to make her understand, but the best he got was "By all means, call me when your butler returns from England. *If* he ever does."

The car roared off down the driveway, rattling across the planks of the twenty-foot-long bridge over the creek at the bottom of the hill.

Griffin fumed and marched back up the steps.

He glared at Loretta. "Do you know what you just did? I've been trying to date that woman for weeks."

"Well, you certainly wouldn't want to make a bad impression on her, then, by giving her your cold. That'd be terrible. She'd be overwhelmed by all those nasty little oxidants, her yin and yang would have a terrible battle, and then where would you be?"

He didn't have a good answer for that as she breezily went back to the kitchen to clean up the spilled tea and make him some chicken soup.

Having Loretta Santana as his butler was definitely going to be hard on his love life.

Damn, he'd vowed years ago—at his mother's funeral—that he'd never put a woman at risk by getting her pregnant. Irrational as it might seem to someone else, that's how he felt. And he'd been especially careful. He'd always played the field, with women who understood marriage and having kids weren't in the cards if they hung around with him.

Now, to his dismay, he had a pregnant woman on his hands. He didn't want to be responsible. But he damn well didn't know how to get rid of her.

Chapter Two

Griffin stretched and untangled himself from the bed sheets. To his surprise he felt a helluva lot better than he had last night. His sore throat was gone, his head clear. Amazing what a good night's sleep could do for a man. Not for a minute did he attribute his miraculous cure to the herbal tea or chicken soup he'd consumed.

He frowned, recalling the scene at the front door last night and his new butler's offhanded dismissal of Aileen Roquette. If it hadn't been for Loretta Santana he might not have awakened alone in his bed this morning.

Rolling to his feet, he strolled to the window. The southern California sun cast early-morning shadows through the oaks and pines that surrounded his property, tinting summer-dried grass to a golden brown. Though less than an hour from downtown L.A., Topanga Canyon had a rural flavor. Along the winding canyon road, houses varied from modest homes to opulent residences sporting ten thousand square feet of living space. His was on the high end of the scale.

Finger combing his sleep-mussed hair, he scanned the redwood decking that circled three-quarters of the house and cantilevered out over the canyon. In a column of cool winter sunlight, Loretta sat cross-legged gazing toward the distant hillside.

Griffin's lips twitched with the threat of a smile. In this light she looked like a cross between a delicate, dark-haired wood nymph and a chubby Buddha. Grimly he remembered he had to find some way to send her back to wherever she had come from.

He grabbed a pair of walking shorts from the closet, tugged them on and strolled outside. The mild air brushed against his bare legs and chest, promising a day that would grow much warmer, even though the calendar read early December.

Leaning back against the deck railing, he crossed his arms over his chest. "Do you meditate every morning?"

Slowly she opened her eyes and a little smile played around her lips. *Kissable lips,* he thought, momentarily caught off guard by her serene expression.

"I learned to meditate while I was working as a temp for the Transcendental Psychic Society. The technique's really helpful to keep your free radicals from escaping." She frowned and shrugged. "Or maybe they're supposed to escape. I forget which. But meditation is really good for you.''

He had the distinct impression Loretta spoke an entirely different language than he did. ''Is the society where you learned about ions and oxidants?''

''No, I learned that while I was working at a health food store.''

She tried to get up but couldn't manage the right leverage. Griffin caught her arm to help her up before she turtled onto her back and was stuck there indefinitely. Her bones were so delicate; how could she carry the extra weight of the baby? He was amazed once again by her hidden strength, and a little bit scared by the risk her pregnancy posed.

Why the heck had she showed up on his doorstep?

''Thanks.'' She flushed, her voice breathy. Glancing away from him, she dusted the back of her dark pants off with her hand. ''I probably would have learned more but they fired me after two weeks.''

''The health food store?''

Nodding, she smiled sheepishly. ''They caught me eating a Big Mac and fries in the stockroom.''

He swallowed a laugh. ''That does seem a little sacrilegious.''

''They could have given me a second chance, though,'' she said seriously. ''I'd only been there two weeks and they shouldn't expect a person to go cold turkey like that when it comes to junk food. I mean, they didn't even want anybody to eat chocolate.''

''They probably had to maintain their standards.''

"That's what they told me." She shrugged, apparently unaware of how that made her breasts rise and fall in a very intriguing way. "I'll get your breakfast now. I've got hand-squeezed orange juice for you, and I sent out early for papayas and strawberries to mix in. That'll get your enzymes back on track."

"I'm fine this morning." Though he'd had an interesting reaction to her reference to *hand-squeezed* which had nothing to do with orange juice. "Why don't you just bring me a cup of coffee and we can sit here and talk a minute."

"Coffee?" She lifted a censuring brow.

"Yes, coffee. Caffeinated, if you please. If you're offended by my asking you to bring me coffee, I'll fix it myself."

"Of course I'm not offended," she said in a huff. "They taught me—"

"—in your accelerated butler classes. Coffee, Loretta. Now."

Loretta hustled into the kitchen. Every bit of the calm she'd managed to gain through her meditation had flown right smack off the deck when she'd opened her eyes to discover Griffin standing there.

A man ought to know better than to show up first thing in the morning practically naked. And then to start giving her orders. For pity's sake! How was she supposed to concentrate while she stared at that broad chest of his with its fascinating swirls of springy brown curls? Or when she surreptitiously glanced at his muscular legs roughened by the same intriguing hair. She wasn't a saint. For heaven's sake, the man gave her ideas she shouldn't even be considering. Not in her advanced state of pregnancy. Not at all, she sternly reminded herself while trying to forget the warm feel of his hand on her elbow, steadying her.

She knew he was a megamillionaire, which didn't trouble her one way or the other. The fact that he'd been plastered on the cover of grocery store tabloids as a big-time playboy did. Maybe she hadn't recognized his name or his face immediately. But the truth had come to her the moment Miss Redheaded-Doll-Face had shown up at the door.

Some impulsive, protective instinct had made her want to close the door in the woman's face. He deserved better than a bit actress who was about to be written out of a minor role in a mediocre soap by the hunky, dark-eyed villain popping her off in a fit of jealous rage. Loretta was certainly familiar with the storyline of the soap in question and could see what was coming.

Griffin Jones would simply have to be more discriminating about whom he dated while Loretta was in his employ. No doubt he would thank her eventually.

Which he would never have a chance to do if she didn't get his breakfast out to him in a hurry and he fired her before he got his mainline morning dose of caffeine. Rodgers had indicated their employer could be a grouch before he got his coffee. Loretta wasn't eager to test the waters.

Minutes later she carried a tray out to the deck—
a generous pot of strong, black coffee, juice and
homemade whole wheat date muffins slathered in
let's-pretend butter. Now was assuredly the time to
impress her boss.

"There you go, sir. The perfect beginning to your
day. Fifty-two percent of your daily minimum requirements for A, C, E, B—"

"It looks delicious." Griffin waved her to sit
down. Breakfast did look good and smelled even
better. He took a sip of coffee. The caffeine jolted
him with a sharp wake-up call, and he relaxed momentarily to enjoy the scenery—including his dark-
eyed butler. "You're not eating?"

"I had my breakfast ages ago. I'm usually an
early riser."

"I see." He broke off a bite of muffin and
watched the steam rise. She might not be acceptable
as an employee of a health food store, but she knew
a helluva lot about baking bread. "Do you live
somewhere, Loretta? I mean, do you have an apartment where you stay when you're, ah, not here?"

"I had a place. After Isabella died I gave it up,
knowing I'd need the extra money. I moved back
home with Mama."

Ah, then she did have somewhere to go if he fired
her.

"Of course, when I learned I'd have this job with
you and would be living here, I gave up my room
to my niece Patrice and her husband. They've got
three kids plus one on the way and needed a place

to stay while they're doing a huge remodeling job on their house. More bedrooms, you know?''

So much for that plan. ''It must be pretty crowded at your mother's house with five additional people.''

''It's not so bad. Of course, she has Enrico there—he's my youngest brother and still in high school. *Tía* Louisa has lived with us for ages. She's my great-aunt twice removed. A wonderful woman who does beautiful tatting.''

''Tatting?'' he asked, distracted.

''It's like lace except stringier. She makes up hope chests full of her tatting for all us girls. For our wedding presents, you know.''

He nodded as if he understood. He didn't. ''So if you went home now—''

''I'd have to sleep on the couch.''

Griffin's eyes crossed. A pregnant woman shouldn't have to sleep on the couch. It couldn't be healthy. Desperately he drained the rest of the coffee from his cup.

''You want some more?'' she asked graciously.

''Yes, please.'' It was more a groan than a request. Dammit all! He was a business executive running a multimillion-dollar corporation with retail stores in the ten western states. This little waif of a female shouldn't have him so far off balance with her whimsical stories, floating oxidants and the feeling *he* was responsible for her. Maybe he ought to hire her to work in one of his stores. That way she'd at least be out from underfoot. ''Tell me, Loretta,

CHARLOTTE MACLAY   31

do you know anything about computers or electronics?''

She poured from the pot on the tray. "Oh, sure. Lots. What would you like to know?''

Relief surged through him. There was a way out of the maze he'd found himself in.

"I play Nintendo with my nephew all the time,'' she continued brightly. "Of course, he beats me most days, but I'm getting better.'' She looked at Griffin with so much enthusiasm, he didn't want to be the one to quash her spirit. But what the hell could she be majoring in to have a hundred and thirty-something units and not know squat about computers? Unless she was putting him on.

"When is your baby due?'' he asked. A hopeless sense of futility settled over him. No way was he going to be able to get rid of this woman.

"Four weeks. And it's only three weeks until I'm eligible for the insurance I need. See how well things work out when God is on your side?''

The headache that had only been a threat last night stabbed him right between his eyes. "You're right." He shoved back from the table. "I've got to go into the office.''

"On a Saturday?'' she gasped.

"Yeah, on a Saturday.'' If it had been Christmas Day, he would have gone into work to get away from the craziness that had invaded his home. Besides, he really did have work to do. He suspected his uncle Matt and his competitive electronics outlets were somehow diverting Compuware shipments to their own Compuworks stores. He needed to track back through the records to see if that was a possibility and if he had a spy in his own firm. The holidays were their busiest season, the sales during the month before Christmas representing a huge percentage of the annual gross. Losses now couldn't be made up later. The industry changed too fast for second chances.

Loretta staggered to her feet, out of balance because of her swollen abdomen. "I put your car away in the garage for you last night. Rodgers said it shouldn't be left out. Vandals and thieves, you know."

"Yeah, thanks. I'll be late getting home. Don't worry about dinner for me." With luck, he might be able to recoup his losses with Aileen.

Upstairs he showered, shaved and dressed casually for his day at work. He hated wearing suits, but the job required it of him when he was dealing with suppliers. Not so on Saturday.

Feeling refreshed, he went downstairs, hit the button for the garage door opener and gazed in dismay at the dented front bumper and broken headlight on his prize Mercedes 450SL.

"Loretta!" he bellowed.

Loretta winced. She'd known he was going to yell at her. She didn't have to like it.

"I'm coming!" She sped up her waddle to a near run, hurrying to the garage. She couldn't remember seeing a man truly glower before, all deep lines and grooves that turned his face into a mask of fury. Not until now.

"Would you care to tell me what happened to my car? My *classic* car?" he added tightly.

"I don't want you to worry about a thing, Mr. Jones. My brother has promised he'll fix—"

"Why didn't you tell me you'd practically totaled my car?"

"Now if you'll just be calm, Mr. Jones. Your electrolytes are going to get all in a flurry—"

"Miss Santana!"

She swallowed hard. "Yes, sir."

"I want to know how you managed to do that much damage moving my car less than a hundred feet from the front of the house where I parked it into the garage."

"I couldn't find the light switch."

He looked at her blankly. "What light switch?"

"For the headlights, of course. I've never driven a Mercedes before. And then when I tried to drive it into the garage—per Rodgers's very specific instructions—my foot got caught in the hem of my nightgown. I was trying to unhook that when I kind of stepped on the gas pedal with my other foot. That's when the potted palm over there practically leaped out in front of your car."

Griffin closed his eyes and drew a deep breath. He was *not* going to lose his temper. Nor was he going to picture Loretta running around outside in the middle of the night in a nightgown.

"You really don't have to worry about a thing,"

she assured him. "Roberto is going to come pick up your car any minute now."

"Roberto?"

"My brother. He does wonderful car repairs. Your Mercedes will be right as rain in no time."

"I think I'd rather take it to the dealership that knows how to handle these classic cars. Thanks, anyway."

"Oh, but Roberto will only charge you half as much as one of those fancy-shmancy dealerships would."

"I've got insurance."

"All the more reason why you should let Roberto do the work. A dealership would overcharge you, and your insurance rates would go up. You'd end up paying two or three times as much as you would if you had just let Roberto take care of things in the first place."

Griffin knew there was a hole in her logic somewhere. He just couldn't put his finger on it at the moment. The image of her dancing around his driveway in a see-through negligee was like a looping videotape in his brain that he couldn't switch off.

"Besides, Roberto is family," she said with the same finality that an archeologist would use to announce he'd found the key to the Dead Sea Scrolls.

He glanced at the crumpled fender and broken headlight. "When is your brother coming?"

"Any minute now. He had to fix his tow truck first."

Somehow that did not bode well for the future.

But Griffin didn't have the time or energy to stand around arguing with his pregnant butler about who was going to repair his convertible—the only car he owned at the moment. "Look, I've got to get to the office. I'll call a cab—"

"Don't be silly. You can use my car. I'm not going anywhere today."

He followed her gaze toward the far end of the four-car garage. A battered compact sat just beyond the last doorway. From what he could see, the vehicle had been cobbled together out of junkyard parts, each fender a different color and a trunk lid that was tied closed with a rope. He never should have sold his Rolls....

"Does it run?" he asked.

"Oh, sure. Like a top. Roberto keeps it going for me." She produced a key from her pocket just as a tow truck came roaring up the driveway, smoke belching from the tailpipe. The driver backed it around, end first toward the damaged vehicle.

Griffin coughed at the fumes. "Maybe we ought to switch to plan B."

"He'll do a wonderful job. You'll see."

Hurrying over to the truck, Loretta gave her brother a hug when he climbed out.

"Hey, sis, is that the guy you're living with?" Roberto asked, eyeing Griffin with the protective instincts of a big brother.

"I'm not *living* with him, not like you mean," she protested.

"Yeah, well Mama's not too thrilled about you

moving in with some stranger. You oughta be home where she can keep an eye on you, Lori.''

"There's no room. Not with Patrice living there. Besides, I need the money.''

"All the same, it just don't look right, you shacking up with some guy nobody knows.''

"I'm *not* shacking up with him. I'm his butler. Besides, he's got so many girlfriends, he wouldn't give me the time of day, even if I were interested. Which I'm not.'' No way could Loretta compete with women like that Miss Redhead person. Not that she'd want to. And given her advanced pregnancy, she didn't imagine any man, most certainly not a well-known millionaire playboy, would give her a second thought. Even if she'd want him to. Which she didn't.

"Any guy would be lucky to have you, sis. Everybody in the family says so.'' Roberto waved to Griffin and called to him. "I'll have your wheels hooked up and outta here in a minute.''

"Fine,'' Griffin said. "Just be careful. I'd just as soon you didn't do any more damage than has already been done.''

"*No problema.* Since you're a friend of Lori's, I'll even give you a tune-up. No charge.'' With another wave, he scooted under the Mercedes to hook up the towing cable, leaving only his overall-clad legs and his work boots sticking out.

Griffin came closer. "Look, I still think it'd be smart to call a dealership. I wouldn't want anything—''

"You worry too much, Mr. Jones. Roberto's practically a genius when it comes to cars."

Her employer didn't look convinced.

Roberto scooted back out from under the Mercedes and hopped to his feet. "Piece of cake," he said with a cocky grin.

He flipped the lever up on the hydraulic lift and stood back to watch. Slowly the rear end of the car rose and edged toward the truck. It was a beautiful convertible, all shining silver-blue with lots of chrome, colors that matched the owner's strikingly attractive eyes. Loretta could hardly believe she'd actually had a chance to drive the car, albeit right into a potted palm.

Griffin's stress level grew more palpable with each inch the car rose above the driveway. He really ought to increase his intake of vitamin E, Loretta concluded. Or maybe it was vitamin B he needed. She'd have to be sure he had plenty of both. Clearly, he was suffering from too much tension in his life.

At the instant that thought came to her, something went wrong with the hydraulic lift. With a pop, oil squirted out, spraying all over the Mercedes and pooling on the concrete driveway. The car shook precariously for a moment, then dropped with a crash, the back colliding with the industrial-strength bumper of the tow truck.

Metal squealed. The Mercedes's bumper twisted, coming lose from its mooring and jutting up at an odd angle.

Cringing, Loretta wished she could crawl into a

hole right there in the middle of the driveway. But
when she met Griffin's furious gaze, she knew that
even a hole dug all the way to China wouldn't be
deep enough to protect her from his righteous anger.

Her only choice was to do a whole lot of fancy
talking. And do it in a hurry.

Chapter Three

Griffin couldn't believe he'd allowed himself to be talked out of having Roberto arrested for assault and battery on his Mercedes. Reckless mayhem, at the very least.

Worse, he'd permitted the incompetent fool to tow his prize car away. Probably to the nearest metal shredder, he thought grimly.

It had been Loretta's tears that had done him in. That and her crazy insistence that he was upset only because his yin and yang had gotten out of balance. What he needed was megadoses of vitamins B and E, she assured him between quivering lips.

Now, how could any reasonable man argue with a combination like that? Particularly when he was scared spitless if she got too upset she might have her baby right there on his driveway.

He pulled into his parking spot at the headquarters

of Compuware, and Loretta's ancient relic of a car lurched to a stop. He turned off the ignition. For several beats the old Datsun kept on chuffing. Grimacing, he hoped no one had seen him drive up. If he had any sense, he'd park it a block away and hope somebody would steal the damn thing. It wouldn't do much for his image as a corporate executive and playboy millionaire to be seen driving this crate around town.

Not that he cared a whole lot, he thought with a grin, thinking about his imp of a butler. He couldn't remember any woman who'd been so unimpressed with his wealth, much less that he was also her employer. Family was the only thing that counted with her—in this case, her brother, her long-suffering mother, *Tía* Louisa and a half-dozen other relatives who were counting on Roberto to help support them with his fledgling auto repair service. A virtual army of loved ones Griffin hadn't been able to fight.

He didn't suppose he had that many relations in the entire universe.

The one he did have—Uncle Matt—wasn't high on his list of people he owed favors. Ten years ago Matt and Griffin's father had had a falling out. A feud had started, eventually ending in Matt breaking up the Compuware partnership to start his own company. In the process he nearly bankrupted the firm. The rivalry was still bitter.

Even so long after the split, Griffin felt a sense of betrayal. Matt had been his favorite uncle—his only one on his father's side of the family. He'd had to remain loyal to his dad but dammit all, neither one of them had given a darn about him. And he'd loved them both.

Griffin used his key to let himself in the door of Compuware's headquarters building, which fronted on Washington Boulevard with the warehouse in back. His footsteps echoed across the empty lobby, and he took the stairs to the third floor.

Almost the moment he'd set foot in his office, Ralph Brainerd showed up.

"Have you seen this, Jonesy?" His executive vice president tossed a copy of an early edition of the *Saturday L.A. Times* on his cluttered oak desk. It was folded open to an advertisement for Compuworks, the competition.

Griffin scanned it quickly. "They're beating our prices by twenty to fifty dollars on almost every item. How can they do that and make any money?"

"There's worse news."

"On a day like this?" A day when he'd watched his Mercedes practically being bent in half? "Why am I not surprised?"

"One of our delivery trucks took a header off an overpass in Simi Valley. Turned about two hundred computers, monitors and printers into scrap."

He swore under his breath. "How's the driver?"

"Battered but okay. He'll be off work a couple of weeks. The truck's totaled. I've called the insurance people."

"Right." Griffin sat down in his swivel chair, tilting it back. The springs squeaked. "So tell me how

come Compuworks undercuts us every time? They
can't be buying from the suppliers any cheaper than
we are.''

A wiry man with the physique of a cross-country
runner, Brainy-Brainerd hooked a hip on the corner
of Griffin's desk. They'd gone to high school together, Ralph the brains of the duo. Later they'd
worked side by side in Compuware's warehouse,
sweeping floors and running forklifts. ''Maybe the
old man isn't interested in making money anymore.''

An unlikely possibility, given the way Griffin's
father had ranted on about Uncle Matt being so
greedy. ''It's like they know what our bottom-line
prices are going to be and knock off just enough to
make it a better deal.''

''Seems that way.'' He weighed a letter opener in
his hand, rolling it back and forth in his palm.

''So how do they find out, Brainy? Who's telling
'em?''

Brainy shrugged. ''You figure we've got a spy?''

''It's possible.'' Griffin only knew for sure that
he'd cut about as much waste as he could from
Compuware's operation, and he still wasn't meeting
Uncle Matt's prices. Any more cuts, and he and
Brainy would be back working shifts in the ware-
house themselves.

''You want me to have advertising gin up an ad
for next week to meet these prices?''

''That would almost be too late in the season to
do any good.'' Leaning forward, he studied the

newspaper spread in front of him. Instead of an array of computers and accessories, he saw Loretta's impish face and innocent brown eyes staring back at him. Her knowledge of computers was limited to playing Nintendo with a nephew. Even in this day and age, a lot of people didn't know computer basics. That thought sparked an idea that would advance his company over the competition.

"Compuware and Compuworks are like two dogs fighting over the same bone. What we need is to develop a new market, people who never thought they would buy a computer. They're scared of the technology, and they don't have much money."

He looked up at his buddy. "I want them to come to our stores to buy everything they need to enter the twenty-first century. We'll offer no down payment, extended credit and hands-on help getting started. If they've even been *thinking* about getting a computer for their family for a Christmas gift, they won't be able to resist our deal."

"We could lose our shirts doing that."

"Or it could give us an edge over Uncle Matt."

He and Ralph talked about the idea for a while, finally deciding to get an advertising campaign rolling in a hurry. With luck, they could draw business away from Compuworks and entice new customers at the same time.

"So how'd it go with Aileen last night?" Ralph asked after they'd concluded their business. He waggled his eyebrows suggestively. "Tell me all, boss man. Is she as good in the sack as she looks?"

"I wouldn't know," he grumbled. "My butler discouraged her from sticking around."

"Rodgers?"

"No, my new butler. Say, you wouldn't know anything about that would you?" Griffin was still having trouble believing the agency would have sent Loretta to him, though once she set her mind on something she was a hard person to discourage.

"Not me. I didn't even know Rodgers had quit."

"He hasn't. He's on vacation."

Ralph gathered up the newspapers from Griffin's desk and the notes he'd taken. "So the new guy sent Aileen away?"

"It's a gal, not a guy."

"Your butler?"

"Yeah."

"You're kidding." Ralph laughed. "Some guys have all the luck. Is she a looker?"

Griffin contemplated the question for a moment. Certainly Loretta wasn't as willowy as Aileen or most of the women he dated. Not as sophisticated, either. She'd probably never been to one of the hot, upscale nightclubs in town. He doubted she'd ever attended theater openings or the Emmy Awards. Yet something about her striking features, dark liquid eyes and easy smile suggested her unique beauty went more than skin-deep.

But she was pregnant with another man's child, he reminded himself. Hell, with another *woman's* child, for that matter. And that made her off limits even if he might otherwise have been interested.

Griffin Jones was a long way from wanting to be tied down with a family, particularly a family with aunts, uncles, cousins and siblings that appeared to multiply faster than a computer virus.

"Let's just say I'm planning to mend some fences with Aileen today," he said. "If I can get her up to my place again, the results will be different this time."

Ralph grinned knowingly. "Good luck, boss man."

When he left, Griffin picked up the phone. If he could convince Aileen to have dinner with him, he'd consider that he'd turned a miserable day into a successful one.

Loretta had just finished cleaning up the kitchen when the phone rang. Drying her hands on a paper towel, she answered in her most professional voice. "Jones residence, the butler speaking."

"Hey, Lori. How's it going?"

"Oh, hi, Brenna," she said, smiling as she recognized her cousin's voice. Stretching the cord across the kitchen, she opened the cupboard under the counter and tossed the paper towel in the trash compactor. "How'd you find me here?"

"Your mom said you had a new job. Is it true what they say about your boss?"

"What is it they say?" As if she didn't know or couldn't guess.

"That he has a string of women from here to New York. Movie stars, showgirls. The whole shebang."

"He hasn't confided anything about his love life to me," she said stiffly. This was definitely a topic she did not want to pursue. Employer confidentiality was the keystone of a butler's success.

"Do you think he's as good in bed as he looks?"

"Brenna!" she wailed. "How on earth am I supposed to know a thing like that?" Though if she allowed herself a brief flight of fancy, she'd guess he'd be pretty terrific. He had nice hands, long tapered fingers. His mouth was particularly tempting, his lips— "Did you call me up just to ask about my employer's love life?"

"No, of course not. Which isn't to say I'm not curious, you understand."

"Naturally."

"Anyway, I called because I've got a really big favor to ask of you."

"Sure, what do you need?" she asked, relieved at the change of subject. Brenna was one of Loretta's favorite cousins. Growing up, they'd lived only a block apart and had played together often, though Brenna was several years older than she.

"You know how Buck loves his football games, don't you?"

"Glued to the TV set every Sunday and most holidays," she said with a laugh. The worst time of Buck's life had been when both the Rams and Raiders had moved away from Los Angeles. No more season tickets to see either team in person.

"Well, he got us tickets to the 49ers on Sunday."

"In San Francisco?"

"Yeah, isn't that great? The problem is, we can't take the kids. I wondered if maybe you could baby-sit for us."

Rodgers had explained Sunday would be Loretta's day off. She'd hoped to use tomorrow to catch up on chores she'd been ignoring, like doing her washing and balancing a perpetually overdrawn checkbook. "I don't know, Brenna. Can't Mama help out—"

"She's already got Patrice and her three kids in the house. They're kind of driving her crazy, I think."

Entirely possible. Patrice's children were particularly active. So were Brenna's two little boys, for that matter. But Loretta enjoyed them. They generally behaved well enough when she got stern with them. And Brenna was one of her favorite cousins. Definitely family. To be asked to baby-sit occasionally was only a small favor, one Brenna would be able to return after Loretta's own baby arrived. Hopefully Griffin wouldn't need her car tomorrow.

"Okay, I guess I can come sit for you—if you can't get anyone else."

"You are an absolute *angel*, Lori. Buck will be so pleased." For a moment Brenna's voice faded as she apparently turned away from the phone, probably to discuss the details with her husband. "Buck says we'll bring the kids by about noon before we head for the airport."

"Noon tomorrow?" How could they possibly

leave at noon, fly to San Francisco and get to the game on time?

"No, silly. Today. We're going to fly to 'Frisco, spend a night on the town and see the game tomorrow. It'll practically be like a second honeymoon."

"No, wait a minute. You can't bring the boys here. This isn't my house. I'd have to ask permission—"

"It's the weekend, honey. If what I've read in the tabloids is true, your boss probably won't be home the whole time. Besides, Roberto said the house is so big, he won't even know they're there. We'll see you in a couple of hours. Love you."

"No, wait!" Loretta listened to the silence that followed the click on the other end of the line until it turned into a dial tone.

She rolled her eyes. It was just a little favor, she told herself. Hardly any bother at all when it meant helping out family.

She could only hope Griffin Jones would feel the same way.

Aileen had taken one look at the car Griffin was driving and icily declined his invitation to dinner, or anywhere else, for that matter. First thing tomorrow he was going to rent something more in keeping with his executive image—and hide the ignition key from Loretta. Either that or rent a Humvee.

Arriving home earlier than he had expected, he noted virtually every light in the house was on. Curious, he opened the front door and stepped into the entry.

A very small person came flying at him at about a thousand miles an hour, clipped him right at the knees, sending him sprawling on the parquet floor. The kid bounced up like nothing had happened and sprinted down the hallway.

"Brian, give your brother back his Power Ranger," Loretta's voice called from the far end of the house.

Griffin struggled to his knees only to come face-to-face with an even shorter person. The youngster stared at him with big, solemn eyes.

"Your brother went that way." Griffin pointed.

Whirling, the kid went running down the hallway, shoelaces flapping. "*Tía* Lori! *Tía* Lori! There's a man!"

Griffin stood. He waited with his back to the wall, alert for another attack. Without a doubt the invasion of his house by a hoard of Lilliputians had something to do with Loretta's family.

She appeared from the direction of the kitchen. Her starched white blouse was wrinkled, her bow tie was missing, and tomato sauce had stained a bull's-eye shape on her belly. "What are you doing here?"

"I live here?"

"Well, yes, I know but—" The two boys appeared behind her, peering around her curiously. "I thought you'd be late."

"I had a change of plans."

"Oh." Her gaze flitted around the entry as if she

were looking for a place to hide the children...or herself. "Would you like some dinner?"

"Whatever's easy." He shrugged out of his coat. "I didn't realize we were entertaining tonight. Care to introduce me?"

"Introduce?"

He nodded toward the two dark-eyed youngsters. "They're family, I take it."

"Oh, the boys! Yes, second cousins, actually." Hooking a protective arm around each boy, she edged them forward. "This is Brian and Cody. Say hello to Mr. Jones, boys."

The youngsters mumbled something that sounded like a greeting. Apparently Cody, the younger of the two, had gotten his Power Ranger back from his big brother. He clutched it tightly in his pudgy hand.

"Good evening, gentlemen."

"My daddy watches football," the younger one announced. "Do you?"

"Not very often."

"Boys, why don't you run back to the other room where you can play. You know, I showed you where my bedroom is. Go on now while I fix Mr. Jones his supper."

"Cody ate two plates full of spaghetti," Brian reported. "He's probably gonna be sick."

"Thank you for sharing that with us," Griffin said.

Loretta spun the boys around like tops and headed them toward the back of the house. "I'm sorry. I really thought—"

"They staying long?"

"Till tomorrow. It was sort of an emergency. But you don't have to worry about a thing. They'll be quiet as little mice, I promise. They're really good boys. A little active, maybe, but—"

Something crashed in the other room.

"Active," he repeated.

"I'll just, ah, see what happened." Smiling weakly, she turned and followed the sound of breaking glass.

Griffin stifled a laugh. To think only twenty-four hours ago he'd led a nice, quiet bachelor's life with a stodgy butler to take care of his every whim and beautiful young women showing up at his door. Now he had Loretta and her family.

Like a short-term prisoner, he thought he might start marking off the days until Rodgers's return.

He followed her into the kitchen and watched as she swept up a broken drinking glass, then banished the youngsters to her room in the back of the house. The kids out of the way, she scurried between the refrigerator and stove, heating some spaghetti for his dinner. Leaning against the doorjamb, his arms crossed, he was trying to figure out what made Loretta tick.

"Have you always been your family's doormat?" he asked.

She stopped mid-stride. "What makes you say a thing like that?"

"Well, let me see…" He began to count off the reasons on this fingers. "My first clue was that you agreed to have your aunt's baby. That's a pretty extraordinary thing for anybody to do and probably means you'll never get your degree. Then you insist I hire your brother—who's obviously incompetent—"

"He is not!"

"—to repair my car. Then, at the drop of a hat, you end up baby-sitting your second cousins for God knows what reason."

She scowled at him, as much as a woman with delicate features could. "They needed my help. They're family. What's so awful about that?"

"They're *using* you, that's what."

"You don't know what you're talking about, Mr. Jones." On the offensive now, she shook a serving spoon at him. "I *choose* to help out my family when they ask because a long time ago they were there for me. You see, I'm not *really* a Santana. I don't even know my *real* name. Or my *real* birthday. My mother abandoned me when I was only three years old. It's one of my first memories and not one I particularly enjoy recalling."

"I'm sorry—"

"You see, the cops found me in a scuzzy motel room with a beat-up old teddy bear, a couple of changes of clothes and two empty boxes of Cheerios. They hauled me off, crying and screaming, to the Santanas' house, because they had volunteered to do emergency foster care. That's the kind of people they are—without so much as a minute's hesitation, Mama and Papa took me in. They didn't ask any questions. They just saw a skinny, half-starved, scared little girl who needed love, and that's what they gave me.''

''That still doesn't mean—''

''Eventually, when it was obvious my own mother wasn't ever going to come back, they adopted me,'' she went on, barely pausing to take a breath. ''They already had four kids to feed and clothe. That didn't matter. They took me in, and I'll never be able to give back as much as they've given me.''

''Look, I understand.'' He tried to move closer, but she was brandishing the serving spoon like a Samurai sword, emphasizing each word as she spoke. Little bits of red sauce dripped onto the floor.

''And I'll tell you something else, Mr. High-and-Mighty. When I'm on my deathbed fifty or sixty years from now and figuring out what I regret not having done, I'm not going to be worrying about not having had enough money or whether I got my degree or not. I'll just be darn happy I did everything I could for my family.''

Her free hand slid across her middle. ''And this little baby is going to know all about love, too, just the way the Santana family taught me.''

Fierce pride and determination shone in her eyes, humbling Griffin with its intensity. Had he ever cared about anything as much as she cared about her family? He didn't think so.

No, he had it all wrong. She was no doormat. In fact, when push came to shove, she would stand up to the world, if that's what it took to defend her family from attack. She'd even risk losing a job she really needed by talking back to her boss.

He had to admire that.

Sniffing the air, he said softly, "I think the spaghetti is burning."

She blinked as though she'd just realized what she'd done, and her eyes widened. "Oh, my, I shouldn't have…I mean…I'm sorry—"

"Don't be. I understand a little charcoal is good for the digestive system." And a strong woman could be a challenge for a man.

Not that he still didn't wish Loretta Santana had landed her butler job with somebody else.

She turned to stir the pot. He headed for the cupboard to get a plate, brushing past her, and then he heard her gasp.

"Oh, my…" Her hand clasped her midsection, her eyes wide, and she nearly doubled over.

"What's wrong? Oh, my God, are you having the baby?" Panic whipped through him. "You can't—"

Shaking her head, she took Griffin's hand and planted it on her swollen belly. "I'm fine. She just kicked me is all. A real whiz-banger. Here, feel."

The heat of her body scorched his hand. He wanted to pull back, but she held him there. And then the baby kicked. A champion soccer player couldn't have connected with any more force.

"There's something in there," he said stupidly. Somehow he hadn't associated her rounded belly with a *real* person, however small. Now, to actually feel the movement, to imagine a tiny foot or hand pressing against his, touched him in a way he couldn't describe and certainly hadn't expected. An odd lump formed in his throat, and the knot of panic in his chest tightened.

"A baby. Maria Isabella Santana. Mari—with an *i*—for short."

He gazed into Loretta's liquid-brown eyes, locked on them, and they wouldn't let him go. They seemed to absorb him in a way he was helpless to resist. The sensation was beyond erotic, beyond anything as trivial as sex. It was more like the universe shifting to a new axis. "Aren't you afraid...I mean, taking on the responsibility of a baby all by yourself?" And the risk of death from giving birth.

"Not really. I'm not sure why her mama and papa had to die. But God has given her to me to raise. That's all I need to know."

The baby kicked again, closer to a caress this time against his palm than a punch, like the sweep of a baby's hand in search of an anchor. At some gut level, Griffin wanted to pledge he'd be there to take care of this baby, too. But he couldn't do that. He owed nothing to Loretta. Or the unknown baby inside her. He wasn't a family man. And he didn't *want* to be responsible. Not when the image of his mother's casket kept popping into his head—and the smaller casket of a little sister he never knew and hadn't wanted.

With a force of will he broke the connection between them and stepped back. He was *not* going to get involved with this woman, her baby or her myriad family members. Loretta was trouble waiting to happen.

It was enough he'd been forced to entrust his Mercedes to her brother.

Chapter Four

His car was green.

Less than a week ago his Mercedes had been a silver-blue bullet in mint factory condition. Now it was...seasick-green.

A combination of bile and fury rose in his throat. *Roberto!*

Griffin slammed the door shut on his rental car, left the Catera sitting in the middle of the driveway, and marched up the steps to his house. The porch light was on, the door locked; no butler—male or female—opened it to greet him.

The calm of the past week and the long hours he'd spent at the office trying to get the Christmas specials put together had lulled him into thinking everything would be all right, that the combined efforts of the Santana clan would not undermine his sanity.

He'd been wrong.

Unlocking the door, he shoved it open and bellowed, "Loretta!"

Eerie silence.

He frowned. What? No little Santana nephews and nieces here to attack him from out of the shadows?

Moving cautiously through the house, he noted everything seemed to be in order—*seemed* being the operative word. When Loretta was involved, he suspected order was only an illusion and certainly temporary.

He found her note in the kitchen, the top one in a stack of several she'd left on the spotless counter. In flowing, feminine handwriting, she said she'd left him a tofu-broccoli casserole—filled with delicious antioxidants—in the refrigerator and gave him a phone number where she could be reached, if necessary.

His frown deepened. This was one night when he didn't want to eat *anything* green. What he wanted was for his car to be silver-blue again.

He reached for the wall phone and punched in the number.

"Marco's Pizzeria, Loretta speaking," she announced in a cheerful voice.

She was having pizza while *he* was stuck with tofu and antioxidants? Give me a break!

"Roberto returned my car," Griffin said without preamble.

"Oh, good. He said he'd get it back to you today. I told you he's practically a genius with cars."

"It's green."

"Green? The car?"

"As in bilious."

"Oh, dear."

In the background someone ordered a large pizza with jalapeños, sausage and double-double cheese. Griffin's tongue burned at the thought.

"That's probably because he's color-blind."

He closed his eyes. There was no possibility he'd be able to count all the way to ten if he focused on the stupidity of having handed over his Mercedes to a color-blind car painter. "Why are you at a pizza place instead of here?" Where he could throttle her in person...or better yet, have her lead him to Roberto.

"I'm helping out my brother."

His fingers flexed in anticipation; a muscle tensed in his jaw. "Roberto?"

"No, my brother Marco. It's his pizza place. He was shorthanded tonight, what with his wife being a little under the weather and his oldest boy wanting to go to a school Christmas dance. So he asked if I could fill in."

"And you said yes."

"Sure. He's family."

Irrationally, it galled Griffin that her family was more important to her than he was, and that her brothers were so quick to take advantage of her. "You already have a job."

"Well, sure, I know that. But you've been getting home so late and I thought—"

"Where is this pizza place of Marco's?"

She gave him an address on Pico Boulevard. "Did you heat up the casserole for your dinner? Or did you go out—"

"I have a sudden urge for pizza, Loretta. Put a pepperoni and mushroom in the oven for me."

She didn't miss a beat. "You want jalapeños on that?"

"No, thanks. I skipped getting a lead-lined stomach when they were passing them out."

Loretta's hand shook as she hung up the phone. Given the phone messages she'd taken for Griffin, she hadn't expected to see him until late. Very late. And somewhere at her feminine core, she was secretly pleased his evening had ended early.

But he did not seem pleased with her...or Roberto, which was understandable. She probably should have reminded her brother to check with someone else before he had the car painted. Fortunately green was generally a nice color.

Though not nearly as fascinating as the silver-blue of Griffin's eyes.

She'd been glad all week that he was working late and they'd had little time together. Since the moment he'd palmed her belly, feeling the baby move inside her, Loretta hadn't been able to look into his eyes without blushing. His simple caress had been the most erotic, most intimate experience she'd ever known. She and Griffin and the baby had been in such close communion, it had been as though they all breathed the same air, their hearts pumping in unison.

Even now the thought of Griffin's hand on her that way brought a new flush to her cheeks.

At the same time, his accusation that she let her family *use* her had stung. She'd begun questioning her own motivations. Could she still be trying to earn her place in the family through good deeds? After all this time, that didn't seem possible. She loved them...and they loved her. If sometimes she worried...

"Hey, Lori, you're getting behind," Marco shouted from the dining room side of the counter. "What happened to my jalapeño and sausage?"

She blinked and gave her head a shake, trying to bring her thoughts back to the pizza parlor. "Coming." She shouldn't be questioning her family's love for her. Or thinking about Griffin's hand and where he'd put it, or where she'd like him to. Or his penetrating eyes. Or the way his lips curved when he smiled and how she'd like to...

Waddling to the refrigerator, she selected two balls of pizza dough, one for the in-house customer and the other for Griffin's pizza. She'd have it ready for him when he arrived, though the tofu casserole probably would have had a more calming effect on him than pepperoni would.

As she rolled out the first ball and tossed it to expand the dough into a circle, she considered sprinkling a little Kava root on Griffin's pizza for its calming benefits. But Marco wasn't likely to have any of the herb on hand.

Arching, she tried to ease the ache in her back and loosen the tension in her shoulders.

Goodness, she could use a whole cupful of Kava herself. Just the thought of Griffin showing up here any minute had her shaky hands tossing the pizza crust in a figure eight instead of a circle.

Griffin found the hole-in-the-wall pizzeria. That his chuffing, exhaust-spewing Mercedes had made it at all was something of a miracle. If the "smog police" were within fifty miles, they'd nail him for sure.

He parked the car and left the doors unlocked in the futile hope somebody would steal it. He considered leaving the keys in the ignition to make it that much easier. But the insurance company probably wouldn't go for that.

His temper was somewhere near exploding when he walked into the shop, but the moment he spotted Loretta in the kitchen, all the anger drained out of him to be replaced by a huge dose of concern.

She'd rolled up the sleeves of her maternity blouse and covered herself with an oversize chef's apron. Her cheeks were flushed; the baby-fine hairs around her face were curled with the heat, and beads of sweat dampened her forehead.

My God! She was practically nine months pregnant. How long had she been on her feet? And what kind of an uncaring idiot must her brother be?

Without pausing in the small, tinsel-decorated dining area with a colorful Christmas *piñata* hanging from the ceiling, Griffin strode into the kitchen. He hooked his hand through her arm. "That's it, Loretta. I'm taking you home."

She gasped, nearly dropping the pizza she'd just pulled from the superheated oven. "Home?"

"My place."

"I can't leave. We've got customers—"

"Forget your customers. Think about your baby."

She gave him a wide-eyed stare, dark eyes without a trace of guile. Eyes that would be nice to look at across the breakfast table...and eyes that would twinkle at night as they went to bed. Together. Thoughts he shouldn't be having.

"How many hours have you been on your feet, Loretta? You look exhausted." When he examined her closely, there were bruises of fatigue under her beautiful eyes. He didn't like that one whit. "That can't be good for you or your baby."

"I'm fine. Really." Using her forearm, she swiped at her forehead, brushing back the wisps that framed her face. "It's only another hour or so till closing."

"By that time—"

"Hey, Lori, what's going on? Is that guy bothering you?"

Turning, Griffin found himself face-to-face with

a bull of a man sporting tattoos on both his meaty arms. "I'm taking Loretta home."

"You aren't taking my sister—"

"Marco, this is my employer, Mr. Jones." She stepped between them like a referee in a boxing ring. "He came to pick up his pepperoni and mushroom."

"Yeah?" Her brother drew out the word in a challenge.

From the scowl on Marco's face, Griffin concluded either Marco didn't like Griffin's pizza selection or he wasn't fond of his sister working for him. Maybe both.

"In less than a month, your sister is going to have a baby. She should be resting, not standing on her feet half the night making pizzas in some hole-in-the—"

"I didn't hear her complaining." Marco glared over the top of Loretta's head at Griffin.

"That's because she's used to letting everyone and their brother take advantage of her." Particularly her brothers.

"No, I don't do that," Loretta objected. Her head swiveled from Griffin to Marco and back again.

Marco lowered his gaze, a flash of concern in his eyes. "You know, if you don't feel so good, you can go home. You're the best sister in the world, and I don't want nothin' bad to happen to you or the kid."

"I'm fine. Honestly."

"You need to get off your feet," Griffin insisted.

"Then who's going to make the pizzas?" they both asked in unison.

Two sets of brown eyes gazed at Griffin, one pair hopeful, the other edgy for a confrontation. Griffin had the feeling he wouldn't be able to win a battle with either of them.

"I really can't leave Marco without anyone to help him," Loretta whispered. Her hand, dusted white with flour, rested on his forearm. Her fingers were slender, her nails cut at a practical length, not chic or sophisticated. He had the outlandish thought her hands would look even better decorated with diamonds and rubies—and that he wanted to give them to her.

Ah, hell! Griffin knew the smart thing to do would be to walk out of there and never look back. But the plea in her voice, the innocence in her eyes, undid his good reason. If he left, there'd be no one to look out for Loretta. She'd work until she dropped...and all for her family.

"You sit," he ordered Loretta. "*I'll* make the pizzas."

"Do you know how to—"

"How hard can it be?"

Loretta sat on a stool beside the counter, providing advice for Griffin's first venture into the culinary world of creating delectable pizzas. Keeping a straight face was no easy matter. In terms of natural talent, Griffin might be found lacking, but his heart was definitely in the right place. Despite his sometimes gruff exterior, he really was a sweet man—a man who would be hard for a woman to resist.

She smiled as the crust he was forming scooted out of his hands for the second time, this time landing on the floor.

He swore under his breath, and she said, "You'll get the hang of it. It just takes practice, that's all."

Picking up a new ball of dough, he mumbled something about "rubbing his head and patting his stomach at the same time."

She swallowed a laugh.

No one had ever been so protective of her, so concerned about her health. It was unnecessary, of course. She was the one who was always helping others and watching out for them. She'd done it all of her life. It wasn't as if they were taking advantage of her. Really, it wasn't.

And she was as healthy as the proverbial ox.

But it did feel good to be on the receiving end of all that concern for a change.

It also felt heavenly to get off her feet, and she sighed, rubbing her back.

"What's taking him so long?" Marco complained, sidling up beside her and speaking softly.

"He's doing the best he can."

"He's the guy you're living with, huh? Roberto told me about him. Mama's not gonna like you doing that."

She grimaced. "I work for him. Temporarily."

"He sure acts like he owns you."

"He's concerned about the baby."

"Yeah, right. Like he doesn't have eyes for you?"

"Don't be silly. Mr. Jones doesn't have any interest in me. He dates gorgeous women. Hollywood starlets." Not that she was all that pleased with the redhead he'd selected, but Aileen was attractive...in a hard-edged way. And unlike Loretta, she didn't have a belly big enough to compete with Santa Claus.

For that matter Loretta wondered why Griffin was here making pizzas with her, instead of out on the town with the sophisticated redhead.

A warm feeling of pleasure waltzed through her midsection before she could stop it. Marco couldn't possibly be right about Griffin being attracted to her. That was just her big brother talking, her reaction only foolish, wishful thinking.

"You're prettier than all of 'em, Lor." Marco leaned over the counter toward Griffin. "Can you hurry it up, fella? I got customers passing out from hunger."

Griffin wanted to come back at Marco with a smart remark...or a punch in the jaw. But he figured if he started a fight or got himself thrown out of the shop, Loretta would take over the pizza making again. He didn't want that.

He managed to get dough to form into a circle and plopped it on the pan. Scooping up a ladle of sauce, he slopped it on the crust. Half of it landed on his trousers.

Now what? he wondered. The array of cheeses,

sausages, peppers and who-knew-what-else was mind-boggling. He'd totally lost track of what kind of pizza had been ordered.

"If you can do the crusts, I can sit on a stool to put on the toppings," Loretta suggested. She smiled encouragingly at him.

He shouldn't have felt so relieved. "You got yourself a deal."

Bringing her stool around to the kitchen side of the counter, she scooted up next to him. By the third pizza, they had a routine going. Roll, toss, spread the crust, was his job. She slopped, spread and sprinkled the toppings, and he put the pizza in the oven.

She sat, looking calm and serene.

He stood, and a trickle of sweat edged down his face and neck. His back began to ache.

"This is as good as a workout," he said.

"You're doing wonderfully well. Marco may offer you a job before the night's over." Her eyes twinkled with amusement, reminding Griffin of stars shimmering in a dark sky.

"Thanks, anyway. I think I'll pass." Though he was secretly pleased by her praise. Which was ridiculous. Anybody could make a pizza. Except he liked doing it with her, liked the way they'd become a team. A well-oiled machine.

Besides, he didn't imagine many women could look so damn sexy sprinkling pepperoni, chilies and cheese on a pasty-white crust. Hell of a way to spend a Friday night.

She didn't seem to mind, though. As customers

came in, she greeted them from behind the counter, asking the kids about their parents, the grownups about their kids. She knew everybody, and they knew her.

They respected her, too. Old and young alike asked for quick words of advice, which she handed out as easily as she scattered toppings on the pizzas they ordered. And they all left the store with a cheerful "Have a good Christmas."

Loretta might be a long way from getting a college degree, but she was a natural when it came to human relations. His store managers could learn a lot from her.

By the time the shop closed, Griffin's clothes were covered with tomato sauce, he'd burned his forearms twice pulling pizzas from the hot oven, and he doubted he'd ever get the smell of oregano out of his nose.

Loretta looked better than when he'd arrived at the shop, less flushed and more relaxed. A small victory.

"Where'd you park your car?" he asked as she untied her apron and tossed it into a laundry bin.

"In back."

"I'll walk you."

"You don't have to do that. It's right outside the door."

"Indulge me. I'd like to see you safely into the car and the doors locked, motor running. This isn't a real good neighborhood."

A sweet smile curved her lips. "I was raised near here, and I know most of the people on the street. I'm probably safer here than you are."

"Fine. Then once you're in the car, you can follow me across the street to where I parked mine. Assuming no one had the poor taste to rip it off."

She called goodbye to Marco, and they stepped out the back door into an alleyway. There was a touch of winter in the air and even a hint of rain. The cool air, after being in close proximity to the overheated pizza ovens, made Griffin shiver.

He held the car door open while she awkwardly got into the compact, her pregnant belly allowing her little room to maneuver between the seat and the steering wheel. At the rate she was growing, in another month she wouldn't be able to get behind the wheel at all.

She needed something bigger to drive, something more substantial. He waited while she got the car started. A big puff of smoke spewed out the tailpipe as the engine caught. Roberto, Griffin decided, needed a new career.

Walking down the alley, the Datsun's headlights lighting his way, he was struck by how dark it was. He didn't like the idea of Loretta being on her own back here and wondered if her brother ever thought to make sure she was safely on her way.

They reached the street and he spotted his car right where he'd left it. Apparently even the local car thieves weren't interested in his bilious-green Mercedes.

Or maybe they hadn't been able to get the thing started, either, he decided after five minutes of futilely trying to crank the engine over and getting no more than a grinding sound.

"Should I call Roberto to pick up your car and haul it back to the garage?" Loretta asked. She'd stayed, waiting for him to be safely on his way. Wasn't gonna happen anytime soon.

"No, it's late. You need to get home and get your rest." So did he, for that matter. "I'll leave the key under the mat. We'll call Roberto in the morning. He can tow it to the dealership, where I should have taken it in the first place."

Studying the car in the yellow glow of the streetlight, she tilted her head in an endearing way. "It doesn't look all that bad."

"It doesn't run, Loretta, thanks to your brother's *free* tune-up. That's one of the basic requirements I have for any car I own—that it goes when I want it to. Even green ones."

"I suppose that's reasonable. But if you leave the key in the car overnight, isn't someone likely to steal it?"

"That's exactly what I'm hoping for," he said grimly.

No more graceful than Loretta had been, he got into her car. The passenger seat wouldn't slide back, so he was forced to fold his knees up under his chin. Little wonder Aileen hadn't wanted to be seen with him in this crate.

Shifting, Loretta applied her foot to the accelerator, eased up on the clutch and the car lurched forward.

"I'm surprised you didn't have a date tonight," she said as she maneuvered through the westbound traffic on Pico Boulevard.

"I was out of the office most of the day. Didn't have time to call anyone."

"Didn't you get the messages from Aileen?"

He frowned. "What messages?"

"The ones I put under the note I left you about where I'd be."

"I didn't read them." He'd been so upset about his car, he'd only wanted to yell at somebody, preferably Roberto. Though he'd ended up taking his anger out on Loretta instead.

"That's too bad. She called a couple of times. Said something about being free tonight."

"Why didn't you tell me when I called you?"

She lifted her chin in a sure sign of stubbornness. "I wrote out her messages very carefully. I assumed you'd read them, since I had gone to such trouble. They made it quite clear in the Butler Academy that I should respect your privacy." She brought the car to a jerky stop at a red light. "How was I to know you didn't read them? For all I know, she might have turned you down and that was the reason you've been in a bad mood all evening."

"I'm in a bad mood because Roberto totaled my car and then painted it putrid green. Wouldn't you be mad about that?"

"No, I like green."

Flexing his cramped shoulders, he tried to get into a more comfortable position. If he'd read the damn messages, he could have been out with Aileen now at some hot spot in town. Instead he'd spent half the night making pizzas. That was crazy!

Then again, if he'd taken Aileen out in his green car and it had died on them before he could get her back home, the night would have been a flop, anyway.

His gaze slid toward Loretta. Driving around in an old junker didn't bother her. In fact, if his guess was right, possessions meant nothing to her. Only family.

Griffin hadn't been raised that way. But he couldn't help admiring her attitude.

They reached his house, the quiet, rural character of Topanga Canyon a far cry from the busy city streets of L.A.

When she'd parked at the end of the row of garages—half of them filled with computer gear he'd built himself—Griffin unfolded himself and got out of the car. Loretta got stuck behind the wheel.

"Here, let me help."

"I'm okay." She grunted and swung her legs to the side, dangling them in the open doorway.

He took her arm. "Have you always been so stubborn and independent?"

"One of my finest..." Grunting again, she came unstuck like a cork from a champagne bottle, and once on her feet, she stumbled against him. "...qualities."

Instinctively he wrapped his arms around her. Except for her bulging midsection, she wasn't very big, but her breasts pressed against his chest in a tantalizing way. His body reacted with a surprising amount of force.

This was his *butler,* for heaven's sake. His *pregnant* butler, and he shouldn't be feeling anything except a desire to go to bed. Alone.

But another kind of desire surged through him like a high-voltage electric charge, one powerful enough to melt a hard drive.

He held her a little more tightly, one hand slipping lower to palm the swell of her hips. Womanly hips. She was made to have a man's babies. Not as a surrogate but with a man she loved, a man with whom she wanted to make a family.

She rested her hand on his chest, right over his heart, and he knew she could feel the beat heavy and hard against her palm. Tilting her head, she looked up at him with dark, curious eyes.

Her full lips were the perfect design for long, slow, deliberate kisses. For tasting and pleasure. For hours of lingering exploration.

He dipped his head toward hers.

She murmured a soft sigh and her eyelids fluttered closed.

Chapter Five

Loretta waited. She couldn't possibly have drawn a breath if her life had depended upon it. Paralyzed by anticipation, she couldn't move.

She waited for the first brush of his lips against hers, waited to feel their warmth and satiny texture. Waited for his tongue to toy with hers, to taste his unique flavor mixed with pepperoni and a sexual need of his own. She waited for what seemed a lifetime, dimly knowing only milliseconds had passed.

Weakness made her legs take on the consistency of cooked noodles, and she leaned toward him. Surely he would kiss her soon. The waiting demanded every bit of her fortitude, her whole body aching for his kiss.

Beneath her hand, his heart beat a rapid rhythm that mimicked her own frenetic pulse throbbing low in her body. His wide palm sent heat through the polyester fabric of her slacks to brand the swell of her hips. Her belly pressed against his midsection.

How much longer would she have to wait?

He cleared his throat. "Loretta, it's getting cold out here. We need to go inside before you catch a chill." His voice was deep and throaty, husky with emotion.

Loretta had never felt such heat, such wanting.

Slowly her eyes opened, returning her to reality as she caught his guarded expression. Griffin wasn't going to kiss her. He'd already stepped away, leaving her swaying without his support.

The ache of need she'd felt became a lump of embarrassment in her throat, and her vision blurred. Why would he want to kiss her when she was already used goods?

"Yes, of course," she whispered, the words as painful as razor blades in her throat.

"You need your rest."

She needed something more than a good night's sleep, but she didn't imagine Griffin would be willing to provide her with the necessary energy boost. And she didn't suppose a huge dose of her favorite herbal supplements would do the trick, either, no matter what they'd say at the health food store.

Suddenly her legs and back ached from being on her feet so long. She wanted nothing more than to curl up in her bed alone and have a full-fledged pity party. But life hadn't dealt her a hand that allowed for that sort of self-indulgence.

She lifted her chin. "Anything special you'd like for breakfast tomorrow?" she asked.

"No, you can sleep in. I'll just pour myself some cereal."

"But it's my job—"

"Loretta! I don't want to hear you stirring until after eight, have you got that?"

She swallowed hard. "Yes, sir."

"I'll be going to the office early in the morning. You won't have to worry about me, okay?"

"Whatever you say, sir." But she did worry about him. He worked too hard; his hours were too long. As nearly as she could tell, lately he hadn't even been dating. A man needed a certain amount of recreation—though she was loath to consider the recreational opportunities a wealthy playboy like Griffin must certainly enjoy.

He placed his palm at the back of her waist, gently propelling her toward the front door. "If your brother Marco needs a helping hand tomorrow, tell him to forget it. You're my employee and I don't want you overdoing it working for him when you're on my time clock."

His gruff attitude didn't fool her. He was concerned about her health, despite what he might say. A warm feeling of contentment eased the lump in her throat.

But that wasn't enough to make her forget her longing to taste just one of Griffin's kisses.

She got ready for bed, then lay staring up at the ceiling, suddenly sleepless as thoughts of Griffin teased through her head like tempting bits of sugar confetti sprinkled on a birthday cake.

A brilliant moon shone into the darkness of her room, making it almost like day, and she could make out the chest of drawers on one wall with a mirror above it and the blank screen of Rodgers's small TV. In her imagination she could see Griffin tossing and turning on his bed upstairs, wanting her as much as she wanted him.

But that was an illusion. Nonsense from an overactive mind bent on self-destruction.

Eventually she slept and woke to a house that was strangely quiet. No creaks, no water running, no electric razor humming as Griffin prepared himself for a day at the office.

A glance at the clock told her she had indeed slept in. And Griffin was gone.

She showered and dressed in her butler's attire— in case someone dropped by and she had to answer the door—then brewed herself a cup of chamomile tea and ate a bran muffin for breakfast. There were no dishes left in the sink, and she assumed Griffin must have gone off without his morning coffee or anything to eat. He really shouldn't do that. With him working so hard, his resistance could weaken. Who knew what kind of bug might attack him if he wasn't careful about his nutrition? She'd have to fix him something extra for dinner, something filled with loads of antioxidants and vitamins.

Leisurely she went upstairs to straighten his room and make his bed. The sheets were a tangled mess, suggesting he'd had a restless night. Secretly she hoped she and their near kiss had been the cause.

She tugged the blankets into place and fluffed the pillow. Griffin's scent was there, a masculine musk that was both erotic and arousing. She held the pillow against her cheek, inhaling deeply. She really needed to stop thinking about her employer in a romantic way. There wasn't much point—

"What are you up to, Loretta?"

She whirled at the sound of Griffin's voice, stumbling backward against the wall. "Oh, my sakes alive! You nearly scared me out of my skin."

"Sorry. I didn't mean to startle you." He gave her a grin that wasn't at all apologetic.

"I thought you were at the office."

"I was, but I left some of my papers here."

She was about to admonish him for working too hard, but when she glanced up at the ceiling, her stomach took a tumble. Her eyes widened.

Above her a motor hummed as a slab of the ceiling rolled back, revealing a skylight.

"Is it supposed to do that?" she asked, amazed.

"Sure. When you stumbled, you hit the switch to open the skylight. Pretty impressive, huh?"

"Yes."

"On a clear night it's great to lie there in bed and watch the stars. Very romantic."

She slanted a glance at his huge bed, imagining lying there with him, the sheets tangled from their lovemaking, Griffin holding her in his arms while the stars glided across the night sky. Definitely romantic. But she was an unlikely candidate for an evening spent in his bed when he had the choice of sexy starlets at his beck and call.

Jerking her imagination back in line, she gave the pillow a good hard whack and placed it back on the bed next to its mate. "You didn't eat breakfast. Would you like me to—"

"I grabbed something at a drive-through on the way to town."

"You really need to stay away from those fast-food places. Your enzymes will get all out of whack and your resistance will go on the fritz."

"My enzymes are in pretty good shape."

So was his physique, she realized. He wore a knitted sport shirt this morning, open at the collar, and hip-hugging jeans that were worn nearly white. His fingertips were tucked into his pockets, drawing her gaze irresistibly to his faded fly. Licking her lips, she decided that the part of his anatomy hidden behind the fly matched the rest of him—big and impressive.

Griffin tossed the pasteup of Compuware's weekend newspaper ad on the foot of the bed and went to his desk to retrieve the charts he'd been working on last night and the diskette he'd saved the data on. For some reason the link between his home computer and the one at the office wasn't working this morning.

Finding Loretta in his bedroom had unsettled him more than he cared to admit. Keeping up a nonchalant facade had been damn difficult when he kept thinking of the way her dark hair had looked in contrast to the white pillowcase, a long, black fall of silk so rich his fingers itched to test the texture of each strand.

He liked her better when she pulled her hair back into a bun; she was less tempting that way. Except that when she pulled her hair back, he found the slender column of her neck equally alluring.

Gritting his teeth, he wondered how much longer Rodgers would be gone.

"How are you feeling after last night?" he asked.

"Great. I slept like a top. How 'bout you?"

"I counted pepperoni slices jumping over a fence to put myself to sleep."

She giggled, a feminine sound that made him think of a Southern belle attending her first fancy ball. He envied the man who would claim her first dance.

He tucked the diskette into his shirt pocket. "No calls from frantic relatives this morning asking you to baby-sit or fill in for them at the longshoreman's local?"

"Not a single peep out of anyone."

"That's got to be a first," he grumbled. "I want you to take it easy today. You know, keep your feet up. Take a nap."

She walked around the bed and fluffed the second pillow. "I just got up. Why would I want to take a nap?"

"Because that's what pregnant women do—sleep a lot." He wondered which side of the bed she liked to sleep on and if she curled herself into a ball or liked to cuddle.

She eyed him skeptically. "You've known a lot of pregnant women, have you?"

"My mother died in childbirth."

"Oh, Griffin, I'm so sorry. I didn't know. How old were you?"

"Ten. But it doesn't matter now." He didn't like seeing the shadow of pity in her eyes, didn't like talking about his mother or how she died. After all these years, the pain was still too raw to bring out into the open. He never should have mentioned his mother. It was something he simply didn't talk about. Except he'd blurted out the words to Loretta.

"It was a long time ago, okay? I just want you to take good care of yourself." He didn't want to feel responsible for another woman's death, however convoluted his reasoning might be.

"Your mother's death must have been very traumatic. Boys have a special relationship with their moms."

"Yeah, well..." Anxious to bring this conversation to an end, he said, "I've gotta get back to the office. Brainerd and I need to go over these projections." He turned and headed out the door.

"Will you be home for dinner?" she called after him.

"I don't know. Probably not."

Loretta's shoulders slumped and she rested her hand on her belly. The poor, dear man. Obviously he'd never gotten over his mother dying when he'd been so young. No wonder he'd been so solicitous of her. She wished there was something she could do to ease his grief.

Picking up the paper he'd left on the bed, she studied the advertisement before she placed it on his desk. Compuware was making a big play for customers who were computer illiterate, which struck Loretta as a good marketing ploy to tap into a huge segment of the population.

She was a business major now at the university, planning to help her brothers and sister grow their respective businesses into franchise operations, and she'd already taken an advanced class in marketing.

Compuware's approach, particularly during the holidays, would make a good term paper—if she were attending classes at the moment—which she wasn't. A loan to Roberto to help him buy tools for his garage and truck-rental business had seriously eroded the stash of cash she'd planned to use for tuition this semester.

Idly she wondered if Compuware's personnel would be as helpful as the ad suggested. Implementing this kind of program was far more complex than simply running an ad with pictures of computers tied with Christmas bows in the newspaper.

Perhaps that's how she could be helpful to Griffin—sort of test market the concept at the point of sale—right in the Compuware stores. Surely if anyone could play dumb about computers, she'd be the one. Not that she was entirely ignorant. Beyond Nintendo games, she was also a whiz at a half-dozen word-processing programs. Working for a temp agency, she'd had to be.

As she pondered the possibility of helping Griffin, the phone rang. Minutes later she had agreed to fill in as a practice customer for her sister's final exam at beauty college that afternoon. Teresa was family, after all. And some day, God willing, she'd have her own string of franchise beauty shops. Loretta intended to be her business adviser. Important relationships like that ought to be kept in the family.

After a full day at the office, Griffin stopped by two different singles bars, thinking he'd look for some action. He sipped a couple of beers, not anxious to get drunk, aware of the interested looks he was getting from the available women in the room. Trouble was he wasn't interested in them.

He kept thinking about Loretta. What if she went into labor and no one was there to help her? What if she slipped on the tile floor in the bathroom and hurt herself?

What if she was curled up in his bed waiting for him?

Anxiety beaded his forehead with sweat. He needed to get home before he went totally bonkers worrying about stuff that wasn't likely to happen and certainly shouldn't be his problem anyway.

But as long as Loretta worked for him, she was his problem. And he didn't know how in hell to get rid of her.

He ate some happy-hour popcorn and spicy

chicken wings, calling them dinner, then left for home.

Saturday-night traffic was heavy on Topanga Canyon Road, a stream of cars snaking along the winding road at a snail's pace. Griffin was relieved when he could finally make a left turn into his driveway and the car rumbled across the bridge, the creek nearly dry this time of year.

He parked the rented Catera in the Mercedes's spot inside the garage, not planning to risk Loretta behind the wheel. The dealership had promised to restore his convertible to its factory-original silverblue color and put the engine back in top running condition by the middle of next week—for a price steep enough to make a dent in anybody's wallet.

Letting himself into the house through the connecting door between the garage and the laundry room, he hesitated a moment to be sure he wasn't going to be attacked by a new set of Lilliputians. Safe for the moment, he followed the sound of the TV playing in the family room.

Loretta created quite a picture. Sitting on the floor Buddha-style, she was watching a show on TV and panting as if she had a bad case of asthma. Even more peculiar, her beautiful hair, the long fall of silk he'd wanted to touch, was frizzed into a black Brillo pad, making her look as though she'd stuck her finger in an electric socket.

Taking it as a personal affront she'd do something so awful, he stepped into the room. "What the hell did you do to your hair?"

She panted three more deep breaths, then used the remote to turn off the TV. She beamed a smile at him. "I got a permanent today. How do you like it?"

Griffin sensed this was not a time when a man should be honest with a woman. "It's...uh... different."

"My sister Teresa did it," she said brightly, patting the poofed-out mess with her hand. "She had her final exam at beauty college today, and at the last minute her girlfriend couldn't be her customer. So I filled in for her."

"Gee, that's too bad. I guess she flunked the test, huh?"

"Oh, no, the examiner loved what she did to my hair."

Griffin hated it. "How long is it going to, ah, stay that way?" Like an oversize rat's nest.

"Just till I wash it out. Teresa didn't put the fixer on, so it's not really a permanent."

"Thank God," he murmured.

"But she said if I decided I liked it this way then she'd give me another permanent, this time for real and she wouldn't charge me a dime. I thought that was very generous of her."

Griffin was horrified.

Settling down on the couch, he was almost weak with relief that it was temporary—she would look like a terrible accident had happened at the beauty shop only until she washed out the damage her sister had done. "I really like your hair long, Loretta."

"You do?" Her doe eyes widened in surprise.

"Yeah, I do."

She met his gaze, and he could almost feel himself slipping into the depths of those eyes, drowning in their liquid warmth.

He swallowed hard. "Sometimes, when the sunlight catches your hair just right, it shines like polished onyx."

Her smile was a little tremulous, like she was about to cry. "That's the nicest thing anybody has ever said to me," she whispered. "Thank you."

"Yeah, well…" Mentally backpedaling, Griffin tried to dig himself out of a hole that was getting deeper by the minute. "You do what you want with your hair. It's none of my business."

Her expression crumbled, and as she turned away he caught the disappointment in her eyes.

Ah, hell! It wasn't his job to keep her happy, but he hadn't wanted to hurt her feelings, either.

As she was struggling to her feet, he asked, "So what were you watching on TV?"

"It's a tape." She popped it from the VCR. "Lamaze training. I borrowed it from the library."

"Lamaze?"

"You know, having a baby in thirty easy minutes, or something like that."

He didn't know much about women having babies—except they could die in the process—but he knew it took a helluva lot longer than thirty minutes to give birth. "Aren't you supposed to have a partner when you do that Lamaze stuff?"

"Oh, I will when the time comes. Teresa says she'll come to the hospital with me, and Roberto volunteered, too."

"So why aren't they going to a class with you?"

"Oh, they're both really busy with their own families. You know how it is. Teresa's got two kids—little sweetie-pies—and Roberto's wife is expecting their third anyday now. We might even be in the hospital together, which would be great, wouldn't it?"

It would be even better if Loretta's family would go out of their way to help her as much as she insisted upon carrying a share of their burdens on her own delicate shoulders.

But Griffin didn't want to get involved. Loretta wasn't his problem—just his *butler*.

Getting up from the couch, he said, "I think I'll get myself a snack."

"I could whip you up a broccoli salad with orange sections and celery if you'd like. It's real healthy."

He waved her off. "I think I'm more in the mood for a peanut butter sandwich."

Slipping the Lamaze tape into its holder, Loretta's mouth watered. She'd like some peanut butter, too. Not that it was on her low-calorie diet, she thought with a sigh.

She'd also like to have a partner to help her with the Lamaze training, which also didn't seem to be in the cards.

Her hands shook slightly as she put the video on

top of the TV. The truth was she was scared. Scared of having the baby alone. Scared of the pain and not having anyone there to hold her. Scared something terrible would go wrong.

A woman needed a husband to help her through childbirth, someone who had as much at stake as she did. Loretta realized that now. If Wayne and Isabella had survived the car accident, she might have felt different. Little Mari was, after all, their child.

But now the baby would be all her responsibility.

Rubbing her palm across her belly, Loretta struggled against the threat of tears that were part joy at the thought of impending motherhood and part fear.

It wasn't good for the baby that Loretta felt so scared. She was sure such powerful emotions could slip right through the placenta, frightening the baby, too. All she wanted her baby to feel was love. *Her* love for the baby God had given her to raise and nurture.

"It'll be all right," she whispered, reassuring the child in her belly.

Like a recurring nightmare, Loretta remembered the press of terror she'd felt when she'd been left all alone in the motel room as a child. Someone had come to help her then. They'd taken her to the Santanas, who had loved her and given her a home.

She swallowed hard.

When the time came for the baby to be born, there'd be someone to help her this time, too. God would see to it.

Chapter Six

By noon on Monday Griffin knew the advertising campaign he and Ralph had created hadn't been the total success they had hoped for. The numbers from weekend sales showed only a minuscule increase over the prior week. And once again Uncle Matt's company had matched or bettered their prices. The holiday shopping season was slipping by and Compuware's market share was dropping like a fragile Christmas ornament falling from a tree.

"Damn," Griffin muttered. "I thought we were onto something big."

"Gotta give it a little more time, boss." Brainerd had been scratching his head over the poor results, too. Neither of them had figured out why the concept hadn't brought folks into their stores by the droves. "There's a lot of people out there who are scared spitless by even the word *computer*. The thought of owning one makes them pea-green.''

"There isn't much time left." He tossed the sales printout on his desk and leaned back in his chair, stretching tense muscles.

He hadn't been sleeping worth a damn with Loretta in the house. He kept thinking of her in Rodgers's room, curled into a ball on the bed, all alone—and he wanted to be there with her. No way should he be having erotic thoughts about a woman almost nine months pregnant with another man's child—never mind that she hadn't conceived in the traditional way.

He shot up from his chair. Dammit! He couldn't sit around all day getting aroused thinking about his pregnant *butler!* There was work to be done, and his whole company was at stake.

"I think it's time we go visit our store managers," he said. "Maybe they've got some clue about why Compuware is still chasing Uncle Matt's Compuworks."

Griffin was dragging by the time he got home. Worse, he had yet to discover why retail sales were lagging. Maybe something was going on in the economy, a huge recession or something that he'd missed hearing about.

"Oh, you poor thing," Loretta said, taking him by the arm as he entered the back door and ushering him into the kitchen. "You look so tired, but I've got dinner all ready for you. You just sit yourself down right here at the table. A good, nutritious meal will fix you right up. I'll have it ready in two shakes.''

Tossing his suit coat aside, he sank gratefully onto a chair. He couldn't recall anyone worrying about him the way Loretta did. Certainly not Rodgers, who was stoic and unflappable in the face of the wildest crisis. And something did smell good here in the kitchen, making the room feel warm and homey. Or maybe it was just that Loretta, even dressed in a butler's penguin costume, could magically turn a house into a home. Not that Griffin wanted to dwell on that particular thought.

Bustling around the kitchen, Loretta pulled a casserole dish from the oven. Something was sizzling on the stove. Griffin hoped it was a two-inch steak, bloodred.

"What's for dinner?" he asked.

She shot him a confident grin. "Veggie burgers with alfalfa sprouts and a lima bean chowder. You'll love them. Great energy food and low fat, too."

He stifled a groan. As far as he was concerned, fat was good. But he was too tired and hungry to argue. Maybe he'd have enough energy later to sneak out for steak and fries.

She served him, and Griffin discovered if he coated the veggie burger with enough ketchup and mustard it didn't taste all that bad.

"Would you like to tell me about your day?" she asked enthusiastically. "Talking about your problems tends to relieve stress and would probably help your digestive system, too.''

Great. Most people took antacids for their stomach problems. He got Loretta and alfalfa sprouts.

''My day would have gone better if I knew why our weekend ad didn't generate more in the way of sales.'' He didn't expect Loretta to understand his corporate problems any more than he could fathom the ingredients of the chowder. He spooned some into his mouth. This was one dish that would never make it to his list of top-ten favorites.

''I know why the ad didn't work.''

Slowly he lifted his head. She'd pulled back her hair tonight and tied it into a knot at her nape, all neat and tidy, the pseudo perm a thing of the past. Her cheeks were slightly flushed from bending over the stove. Even without makeup, her lips looked kissable.

He jerked his thoughts away from that dangerous path back to the subject at hand.

''With all due regard, sweetheart, how would you know why Compuware's ads aren't working?'' He and Ralph sure as hell hadn't been able to figure it out, and they had a dozen years in the business.

She pulled up a chair opposite him, sat down and propped her elbows on the table, resting her chin on her fists. ''Because I visited two of your stores today.''

''You did?'' He nearly choked on a lima bean.

''*And* I dropped by a couple of Compuworks stores, too.''

"Why the hell did you do that?" She'd betrayed him. By going to the competition, it was practically like having a spy right in his house.

"Comparison shopping, that's why. It's a well-proven technique to find out what's really going on in the marketplace."

"You don't even know anything about computers."

"Of course I do. But your store clerks didn't know that. I played it real dumb."

Griffin was beginning to think he was the one who was suffering from a bad case of the dummies. "Let's start over. Now you're telling me you're an expert on computers?" Hell, she couldn't even beat her nephew at Nintendo—or so she'd told him.

"Well, no, not an expert exactly. But I can certainly tell when some computer geek is trying to pull a fast one on me."

His interest piqued, Griffin laid down his spoon. "What did the sales person do?"

"Well, this one guy at your Santa Monica store tried to sell me a computer that had less than four gigabytes. I told them I wanted a computer just for family use, for the children, I said. But the one he tried to sell me didn't even have a modem. How would my children ever get on the Internet to do their homework?"

"You don't have any children," he pointed out. Though that situation would soon be altered, her baby wouldn't be ready for a computer—modem or not—for a couple of years.

She ignored his remark. "The salesman really should have guided me toward a configuration that would at least grow with the kids."

"Yes, he should have." It was also obvious Loretta knew more about computers than Griffin had thought. Perhaps the business about losing at Nintendo had gotten him off track. But if that was the case, why did she have such a shaky employment record? And why was she working now as his butler?

"And then at the downtown store, I practically had to tackle a clerk to get him to answer my questions—and I'm in no condition to wrestle anyone to the ground. He had a serious chauvinistic attitude, helping the men who came into the store before he said so much as boo to me. He must not be aware women are involved in making the buying decisions in 78 percent of all big-ticket items."

"Seventy-eight percent? Where'd you get that number?"

"Oh, it's an educated guess. Everybody knows women make the final decisions on most car purchases, and they buy practically all the books these days, not just romance novels. They buy action-adventure, sci-fi, the whole gamut. The only thing men buy a lot of is perfume and that's because they don't know what else to get their girlfriends for Christmas. That's why there are all those sexy perfume ads on TV during the holidays. It appeals to their libidos."

Griffin wasn't sure how they'd gotten from buying computers to marketing perfume.

In a quick gesture, she curved a loose strand of hair back behind her ear, distracting him yet again and drawing his attention to the porcelain shell. A perfect spot to place a kiss, to explore with the tip of his—

"By the way, as nearly as I could tell, nobody in that store could speak Spanish. You're losing sales by not having a bilingual staff. There weren't many women working, either. Sometimes it's easier for a woman to ask another woman a dumb question instead of looking stupid in front of a man."

Frowning as much at his own wayward thoughts as Loretta's revelations, Griffin leaned back in his chair. He'd been to both of those stores this afternoon and hadn't detected the problems Loretta had identified. Nor had his store managers had a clue. He wondered if she'd imagined the failings of his employees.

"Furthermore, at Compuworks they gave me an easy-to-understand list of what to look for when you're buying a computer, plus they sat me down while I read it and brought me a cup of coffee. Of course, in my case, a decaf or nice herbal tea would have been better, but it was a nice thought."

Griffin's frown turned to a scowl. How could she have learned so much in a half day and still had time to fix his dinner? And look so sexy in the process.

"What I think you ought to do," she said, leaning

PLAY TIC-TAC-TOE

FOR FREE BOOKS AND A GREAT FREE GIFT!

Use this sticker to **PLAY TIC-TAC-TOE.** See instructions inside!

THERE'S NO COST*NO OBLIGATION!

Get **2** books and a fabulous mystery gift! **ABSOLUTELY FREE!**

Turn the page to play!

Play TIC-TAC-TOE and get FREE GIFTS!

HOW TO PLAY:

1. Play the tic-tac-toe scratch-off game at the right for your FREE BOOKS and FREE GIFT!

2. Send back this card and you'll receive TWO brand-new Silhouette Romance® novels. These books have a cover price of $3.50 each in the U.S. and $3.99 each in Canada, but they are yours to keep absolutely free.

3. There's no catch. You're under no obligation to buy anything. We charge nothing — ZERO — for your first shipment. And you don't have to make any minimum number of purchases — not even one!

4. The fact is, thousands of readers enjoy receiving books by mail from the Silhouette Reader Service™ months before they're available in stores. They like the convenience of home delivery, and they love our discount prices!

5. We hope that after receiving your free books you'll want to remain a subscriber. But the choice is yours — to continue or cancel, any time at all! So why not take us up on our invitation, with no risk of any kind. You'll be glad you did!

YOURS **FREE** A FABULOUS **MYSTERY GIFT!**

We can't tell you what it is... but we're sure you'll like it!

A FREE GIFT — just for playing

TIC-TAC-TOE!

DETACH AND MAIL CARD TODAY!

With a coin, scratch the gold boxes on the tic-tac-toe board. Then remove the "X" sticker from the front and affix it so that you get three X's in a row. This means you can get TWO FREE Silhouette Romance® novels and a **FREE MYSTERY GIFT!**

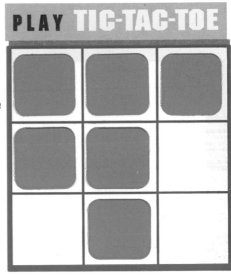

PLAY TIC-TAC-TOE

YES! Please send me the 2 Free books and gift for which I qualify. I understand that I am under no obligation to purchase any books, as explained on the back of this card.

315 SDL CX7T

215 SDL CX7M
(S-R-12/99)

Name:
(PLEASE PRINT CLEARLY)

Address: Apt.#:

City: State/Prov.:   Zip/Postal Code:

The Silhouette Reader Service™ — Here's how it works:

Accepting your 2 free books and gift places you under no obligation to buy anything. You may keep the books and gift and return the shipping statement marked "cancel." If you do not cancel, about a month later we'll send you 6 additional novels and bill you just $2.90 each in the U.S., or $3.25 each in Canada, plus 25¢ delivery per book and applicable taxes if any.* That's the complete price and — compared to the cover price of $3.50 in the U.S. and $3.99 in Canada — it's quite a bargain! You may cancel at any time, but if you choose to continue, every month we'll send you 6 more books, which you may either purchase at the discount price or return to us and cancel your subscription.

*Terms and prices subject to change without notice. Sales tax applicable in N.Y. Canadian residents will be charged applicable provincial taxes and GST.

If offer card is missing write to: Silhouette Reader Service, 3010 Walden Ave., P.O. Box 1867, Buffalo, NY 14240-1867

BUSINESS REPLY MAIL
FIRST-CLASS MAIL   PERMIT NO. 717   BUFFALO, NY

POSTAGE WILL BE PAID BY ADDRESSEE

SILHOUETTE READER SERVICE
3010 WALDEN AVE
PO BOX 1867
BUFFALO NY 14240-9952

NO POSTAGE
NECESSARY
IF MAILED
IN THE
UNITED STATES

forward, "is visit your stores incognito. Then you'd find out just how good your advertised service really is."

"That won't work. They'd recognize me in a minute. I met with the store managers this afternoon."

"But not the clerks, I bet. If you dressed kind of scuzzy and we went as a couple, they'd never recognize you."

"A couple?"

"You know, I'll be your wife."

Wife? She gazed at him with dark, guileless eyes, but he still didn't think it was a good idea. Even pretending to be married was a scary proposition for Griffin—particularly when the woman looked like she was ready to go into labor at any minute.

He shook his head. "I don't think so."

"Well, I could be your girlfriend, I suppose. But I am pretty pregnant for just being a girlfriend. Somebody might get the wrong idea. About us, I mean."

"You're worried about your reputation?"

"Yours, too. You have an image to maintain—if they do recognize you. You wouldn't want people to think you didn't take responsibility for what you've done."

"I haven't done anything." Certainly he hadn't been the one to get her pregnant. And if he had, he sure as hell would have done it the old-fashioned way. None of this surrogate business for him.

"Well, no, but people won't know that by just

looking at us. I think we ought to say we're married."

Griffin did a mental blink. Loretta Santana was capable of more convoluted reasoning than any person Griffin had ever met. Whatever her college major might be, she'd skipped the class on logic.

But some of what she was saying made an odd kind of sense—though not the marrying part. If the problem with sales stemmed from store employees not doing their jobs right, he ought to know that—and hold the store managers' feet to the fire to improve their training. Admittedly, he and Brainerd hadn't given that possibility any thought. They should have.

Cocking his head, he wondered how a tiny woman with big doe eyes and too many relatives had come up with the idea.

"Just what is your major when you're in school?" he asked.

She lifted her chin to a proud angle. "Business. I'm going to specialize in turning small companies into franchise operations—like Roberto's garage and Marco's Mexican Pizzeria." She rested her hand on the swell of her stomach. "Of course, with the baby and all, it may take me longer to achieve my goals than I had hoped."

To his amazement, given the right set of circumstances and legitimate opportunities, he thought she might be able to pull it off—though he had serious doubts about Roberto even being able to make a living as a mechanic. She was certainly determined enough and so stubborn she didn't easily take no for an answer. While he might not think she had a great future as a butler, his admiration for Loretta's business sense went up a notch.

Biting into his veggie burger, he decided letting it grow cold had been a serious mistake. Mustard on cardboard ranked way down there on his list of gourmet treats.

"Okay, I'll make you a deal, Miss Franchise-Expert. We'll try it your way. I'll go incognito with you to a couple of our stores tomorrow."

She smiled her approval.

"*If,*" he added, "you'll let me barbecue the biggest, juiciest steak I can find for our dinner tomorrow night."

A giggle erupted, making her sound young and playful. "And I'll do baked potatoes—sour cream, butter, bacon bits, the whole nine yards." She threw up her arms in surrender. "Who cares about those ol' calories and oxidants, anyway? It's time we lived a little. Cellulite, here we come!"

For the first time in a long while, Griffin was eager for tomorrow to arrive—and it had little to do with business or the evening's menu.

The parking lot at the Santa Monica store was nearly empty when Loretta pulled her Datsun into a slot. She turned off the key, and the car coughed twice before shuddering into silence.

"Here we are," she said brightly. "See, my car got us here just fine."

"If you don't count the two times the engine died, one of which was in the middle of the busiest intersection in town. We're lucky we weren't killed by that trucker you blocked."

"Oh, pooh." She waved off his complaint as unimportant. "The poor man was probably just having a bad day. He didn't mean all those nasty things he said."

"Trust me, Loretta. Guys with that many tattoos and arms like beer kegs mean every word they say."

"You forget my brother Marco has tattoos, and he doesn't intimidate me a bit." Grinning, she squeezed out from behind the wheel and stood.

Using her car had been part of her incognito plan. To go along with her scheme, Griffin had worn ragged cutoffs that displayed well-muscled legs roughened by pecan-brown hair. His gray T-shirt was shorn above the waist and the sleeves were ripped out; he'd intentionally mussed his hair and neglected to shave, leaving whisker stubble on his cheeks. The unkempt combination made him look like the world's sexiest beach bum. Which had seemed to irritate that truck driver no end.

In contrast, her simple maternity dress made her look as though she bought her wardrobe from a tent maker. Fortunately that same truck driver had a soft spot in his heart for pregnant women or they might have been faced with an eighteen-wheeler rolling over the top of her tiny Datsun instead of having the man gently push them by hand out of the intersection.

She swallowed hard as they walked up the steps into the Compuware store. The way she looked, little wonder Griffin hadn't wanted to pretend to be her husband. She was as big as a house and waddled like an overfed elephant. As far as she could tell, his type of woman was long, lanky and elegant, something she'd never been, even on her best days.

Pity the health food industry didn't have a cure for short and stumpy.

He held open the door for her as they entered the store. Red, white and green metallic crepe paper streamers looped across the room, and big red bows were tied around stacked boxes of mock merchandise to create a holiday atmosphere. In the background, Christmas carols played over the in-store music system.

Racks of computer games, software manuals and computer accessories were located up front near the cash registers. The display computers, monitors and printers were in the back; expensive laptops were stored in locked glass cabinets along a side wall to protect against shoplifting. But the hoped-for hordes of customers were missing.

Loretta and Griffin wandered toward the back of the store. Her hand accidentally brushed his, sending a warm spiral of awareness up her arm. He was an amazingly virile man, and whether he was dressed in a suit or in cutoffs it made little difference. A woman couldn't help but notice—or be flattered to be walking at his side.

Though a couple of clerks—one of them wearing

a lopsided Santa hat—were chatting with each other about professional football teams, no one approached them to offer assistance.

"Were either of those guys the one you talked to yesterday?" Griffin asked under his breath, frowning.

She looked over her shoulder. "No, I don't see him. Maybe he has today off."

When they'd strolled the length of the aisle, pretending to study several different computers, and still no one offered assistance, Griffin called to the store clerks. "Hey, could we get some help here?"

"Be right there," the one with the Santa hat replied, but he didn't exactly hurry in their direction.

By the time the jerk finally reached them, Griffin's mood had gone from mad to downright furious, and the kid's condescending attitude toward Loretta had him ready to fire the guy right on the spot—forget any holiday spirit of goodwill. By gritting his teeth, he managed to hold his temper in check until they got back outside.

"I can't believe those guys," he muttered as they walked to Loretta's car. "I'm busting my butt to keep the business in the black and those characters are *sitting* on their butts. Were they like that yesterday?"

"Pretty much," she said.

"Damn, when I was meeting with the store manager, everybody was hustling like they're supposed to." He caught her by the arm and lifted her chin with his finger. "If you hadn't done your impromptu comparison-shopping study, I would never have spotted the problem. I owe you, Loretta.''

Impulsively he bent his head to brush a quick kiss across her mouth. The contact was brief and innocent, yet the warm caress of her lips, fitting so perfectly with his, jolted Griffin. His heart lurched; his mental equilibrium slid off kilter.

Damn, this woman was potent! He hadn't realized...

He stared at her, their faces only inches apart, her eyes wide with surprise, her pupils dilated. Her lips were slightly parted as though she was about to speak—or wanted him to kiss her again. More deeply this time.

His whole body trembled with indecision, a gut-wrenching tug-of-war between desire and good sense. He wanted to kiss her again, and that was a bad idea. Messing with a pregnant woman with soulful brown eyes could only lead to commitment and taking responsibility for her well-being. No more playing the field. No way to keep his emotions in check. He'd be vulnerable, at risk in ways he couldn't handle.

Ways that scared him to death.

Play it cool, he ordered himself, backing off.

''Come on, let's see if this jalopy of yours can get me to the office in one piece. I'm calling an emergency meeting of store managers for first thing tomorrow morning. We're going to get our employees hopping before we blow the entire Christmas season.''

She blinked at him. "Aren't you..." She clamped her mouth shut but didn't budge. "You need to visit a Compuworks store to compare—"

"I don't need to see my uncle's operation to know he's beating the socks off me."

"Your uncle owns Compuworks?"

"You're darn right he does."

"But that's your major competition, and he's family," she said, astonished.

"Yeah, right. Family." He yanked open the passenger door. "Some of us don't feel that we owe our right arm up to the elbow to our family, okay?"

No, Loretta didn't think that was okay. There was nothing in the world more important than family to her, probably because she'd been abandoned by her own. When Mama and Papa Santana adopted her, she'd been so grateful to have a family, she would have willingly given them both of her arms. She still felt that way, still troubled by the niggling feeling that if she didn't give enough, do enough—or demanded too much in return—they might stop loving her. That wasn't true, of course. She'd never had reason to doubt the love of her adoptive family. Even so, she tried to make herself as valuable, as important, to her family as she could, rather than risk losing what she so desperately yearned to be a part of.

"I don't understand why you and your uncle aren't helping each other instead of duking it out in the same business."

He took a deep breath, obviously troubled by her

question. "My dad and Uncle Matt were in business together until Uncle Matt screwed Dad."

"His own brother?" She was shocked. "How did he—"

"I don't know the details. Dad wouldn't talk about it. But about ten years ago they split the company right down the middle and became competitors. It's been a bloody fight for market share ever since."

"Don't you think you ought to know why the breakup happened? Maybe there's a way the two of you could—"

"Loretta, I haven't seen or talked to my uncle in ten years. I'm not about to go knocking on his door now. That'd be like betraying my dad. I can't do that."

A man's pride was a terrible thing. If Griffin's uncle Matt was anything like his nephew, that meant there were tons of that useless emotion on both sides of the family. What a terrible waste.

Walking to the driver's side of the car, she opened the door, sucked in her large belly as best she could and eased behind the steering wheel. Her lips still tingled from the brush of Griffin's kiss, and his faint flavor lingered. He'd meant the kiss only as a thank-you, nothing more. The fact that her heart had done a somersault was her problem, not his. Their relationship was strictly professional—except for that one brief kiss.

But she did owe him her very best efforts.

She slanted him a glance as she drove out of the

parking lot. Given her background, she was an expert on family matters. Perhaps, in addition to her business expertise and talents as a butler, she ought to give Griffin the benefit of her wisdom in that arena, too. Certainly no harm would come from re-uniting an uncle and his nephew. And the holidays were a perfect time for families to put old disagree-ments aside, to forgive and forget.

If she could figure out how to get them together.

Except for the steak dinner he and Loretta had shared, Griffin wasn't home much at all for the rest of the week. When he wasn't in long meetings at his office headquarters, he and Ralph were both on the road visiting their other stores in the ten western states. Griffin was damn well going to see to it that his employees were the best trained in the country, eager to sell the products they stocked, or they'd find themselves in the unemployment line before the hol-idays were over.

In some ways he was glad he hadn't had to face Loretta. Which didn't mean he'd stopped thinking about her and the kiss they'd shared. Or the fact that she was at his house alone and could go into labor at any moment. Who would she call? Which of her relatives would take the time to drive her to the hos-pital?

Fearing that she wouldn't be able to get help any-where else, he'd given her his cell phone number.

Damn, like a disease taking over his immune system, he was spending as much time worrying about Loretta as he was Compuware.

By Sunday morning Griffin was beat and he slept late. Finally rolling out of bed around ten, he went into the bathroom and grimaced at his image in the mirror. This business executive routine was turning him into an old man.

Though it was kind of chilly and overcast outside, he pulled on a pair of shorts and an old T-shirt, then went in search of breakfast.

What he found was Loretta in the kitchen surrounded by what looked to be a thousand pounds of potato salad with more pots boiling on the stove.

"I gather you're planning to feed an army," he said.

She glanced over her shoulder. Her sleeves were rolled up to her elbows, sweat beaded her forehead, and a damp strand of dark hair had come loose from the bun at her nape to cling to her cheek. She grinned at him. "Close to it. The family's having a picnic to celebrate Mama's birthday."

The family. Somehow he should have known. And only in L.A. would a family plan an outdoor picnic in December and have a pretty fair chance of pulling it off without rain or snow canceling the event. The chamber of commerce had to love it.

"Couldn't somebody else have brought the food?" he asked.

She wiped her hands on a towel, then rubbed her back. "Oh, it's a potluck. We all bring something. Teresa's got the enchiladas, Roberto's wife is doing a winter-fruit salad, and Marco's bringing pizza, of course.''

"Yeah, but you shouldn't be on your feet so long. You must have been at this for hours."

"I'm almost done."

From the bruised look under her eyes, she was almost *done in*. "Sit, Loretta," he said with a resigned sigh. "I'll take over from here."

"But I—"

"Just tell me what to do."

He held out the chair for her, and she sat, groaning softly. She rested her hands on her belly. "Thanks. There's not much left to do—just cutting the onions and jalapeños into the potatoes, then mixing it all together."

"Right." Damn it! Somebody ought to be taking care of her. She wasn't his responsibility. But there didn't seem to be anyone else stepping forward to handle the job.

"How'd all your business meetings go?"

"Great." His eyes started to tear the minute he cut into the yellow onion. "We've got a new motto—Compuware, the friendly store where no question is too hard or too easy. Expert or beginner, we're here to help you."

"That sounds wonderful."

He wiped his tearing right eye with his shoulder. "It will be if our employees follow through on the training—or rather the dressing down we gave them this week."

"I'm sure they will. I'll comparison shop a couple of the stores next—"

"You don't have to do that. We've hired a professional shopping company to check our stores regularly."

"I wouldn't have minded."

"I know," he said softly. Glancing at her, he could see how tired she looked, the circles dark beneath her beautiful, soulful eyes. "Are you sleeping okay?"

She shrugged, smiling wryly. "It's a little hard to sleep when there's a soccer game going on inside your belly. I think Maria Isabella Santana may be the first woman to play professionally."

His chest tightened with fear and another emotion he couldn't quite name. "What does the doctor say?"

"I saw him Wednesday. He says I'm fine and so is the baby."

"How much longer?"

"I'm still two weeks from my due date. If it weren't for needing the insurance money, I'd be happy to get this over with anytime little Mari is ready to make her entrance into the world." She patted her stomach. "As it is, she'll probably organize a championship game in the hospital nursery."

"She'll be a winner...like her mom."

Her eyes started to glisten. "Do you suppose she'll call me Mommy?"

"Probably. Or Mama."

"I want to be the best—" Her voice caught.

"You will be." Swallowing hard, he turned back to the onion he was dicing. It was only the fumes that caused new tears to form in his eyes, and being surrounded by a mass of potatoes was the reason he had a lump in his throat. Loretta would be just fine; the doctors nowadays knew what they were doing. And Griffin would damn well see to it that her relatives got her to the hospital in plenty of time.

He finished the chopping and dicing and mixed mayonnaise into the concoction while Loretta changed clothes for the picnic.

"I really appreciate your help." She'd put on a colorful maternity blouse and matching royal-blue pants, and carried a lightweight windbreaker against the threat of rain. A touch of makeup made her look more rested than she had minutes ago—and even more appealing. "Now all I have to do is put these bowls in my car and I'll be all set to go."

"I'll carry them out for you."

"I can manage. They aren't very heavy."

"Maybe not, but balancing them on your stomach is going to be quite a trick."

She giggled. "You may be right about that. I haven't gotten a good look at my feet in weeks."

It took him two trips to juggle the bowls of potato salad out to the car and secure them in the back seat so they wouldn't slide around if she came to a quick stop.

He stood back while she started the car—or tried to. "If you get to feeling tired, you'd better come on home and rest. One of your relatives can hang on to the bowls for you.''

"I will.'' She cranked the engine over, the car backfired and died. Smoke billowed up from the tailpipe.

Griffin frowned.

She gave it another try. This time the engine chuffed and caught, rocking as it continued to misfire on one cylinder. She put it into gear, gave Griffin a jaunty wave and accelerated for about ten feet before it quit again.

Griffin rolled his eyes. He didn't trust Loretta's old car to get her safely to the picnic, much less back home again. And, given her driving record, he sure wasn't going to lend her his Mercedes, which he had just gotten back from the dealership. He didn't even trust her not to work herself to the bone at the picnic trying to serve everybody and their cousin.

Nope, he was fresh out of choices.

"Get out, Loretta. You're going to have a guest for that family picnic of yours and we're taking *my* car.''

Chapter Seven

"Hey, Lori!" A gray-haired man shouted and waved from halfway across the park. "You're late. We thought maybe you'd already had the baby."

"Not yet, Uncle Barry," she called back to him.

"You'll let us know when, huh? I'm gonna be the baby's favorite uncle and spoil her the way I did you."

Loretta laughed. "Mama will call you, I'm sure."

"Is it going to be a girl or a boy?" a preteenage girl with a ponytail wanted to know.

"A girl."

"Lucky you! Boys are the pits." She eyed Griffin, then smiled coyly. "Most of them, anyway."

"Becky, I think Mr. Jones is a little too old for you to be flirting with."

Her cheeks flamed red. "Well, he's a lot better-looking than the boys my age!" With that, she turned and went running off to join a gaggle of her peers.

Loretta laughed as Griffin helped her get the potato salad out of the car. "In another year or two, Becky will very likely change her tune about the boys in her crowd," she said.

"Funny, I thought girls were pretty gross until I hit thirteen. Then I had a change of heart."

She eyed him over the top of a bowl of potato salad. "I imagine from the time you entered kindergarten, every girl in school had a crush on you."

He shrugged. "Along about third grade, Beverly Zumkeller wanted to play doctor and nurse with me behind the cafeteria."

Her eyes widened. "And did you?"

"A gentleman never tells tales out of school."

Her warm laughter cascaded over him as if the sun had come out from behind the clouds. Smiling, her dark eyes dancing with amusement, she turned and headed toward the crowd of her relatives.

Griffin followed with only mild enthusiasm. Family reunions weren't exactly his thing.

Someone had evidently come to the park early and staked out a half-dozen picnic tables, which they'd arranged in a ragged circle. At least Loretta hadn't volunteered for that job, too, Griffin thought, still wishing he could shield her from a family that seemed determined to take advantage of her.

Dozens of people were milling around the tables, laughing and talking all at once while a boom box played jazzy Christmas carols at full blast. On a nearby grassy area, a group of men and boys had started a soccer game; a couple of disinterested teenagers were tossing a Frisbee back and forth. Beneath an old oak tree, a young mother had safely corralled her toddler in a portable playpen, although the baby didn't seemed entirely pleased with the arrangement.

Griffin didn't imagine he had this many relatives in the entire world—a couple of cousins and an uncle he hadn't seen in ten years were about the limit of his family ties.

He placed the two bowls he was carrying on a table already loaded with food and took the third one from Loretta, putting it at the other end of the table. The Santana clan apparently was not only prolific, they also enjoyed eating.

"Hey, Mr. Jones." Roberto came up to him, extending his hand. "Your car looks real good. Nice paint job, huh?"

"Yeah, it's fine now that it's back to metallic-blue again."

Squinting, Roberto looked toward the car. "Funny, I thought your car was green. Oh, well..." He shrugged.

Griffin winced. No way would he let Roberto within ten feet of his Mercedes again, not in this lifetime.

Shifting his weight from one foot to another, he waited while a half-dozen different women hugged Lori, buzzing excitedly about the baby, asking when it was due and telling how long their own first labors had lasted. Griffin wasn't interested in their child-birth horror stories.

He had one of his own that still tortured him— the death of his mother.

Jamming his hands in his pockets, he wondered if he ought to simply take off and come back for Loretta after the picnic was over.

She hooked her arm through his. "I'm sorry. My family can be a little overwhelming sometimes. And everyone seems to think my baby is their own per-sonal project. Poor Mari really is going to be spoiled rotten."

"That's probably because they all love you so much."

A flush of color stained her cheeks. "They're calling her a miracle baby...for the family."

Griffin figured Loretta was the miracle, if not a full-fledged saint. He didn't exactly qualify as the perfect escort.

"Would you come meet my mother?" she asked.

"Look, maybe I ought to just go—"

"I'd like you to stay." She held his gaze for an instant, hope in her warm velvety eyes, then glanced away as though she was afraid to reveal too much. "But I'll understand if you have work to do. I'll catch a ride home with—"

"I'll stay." He didn't belong here, but strangely he didn't want to leave, either. Normally he wasn't this indecisive. But then, he'd felt off balance since the night he'd come home to discover Loretta was his temporary butler.

Her smile lit her eyes, and it was enough to make him glad he'd agreed to hang around. Somebody, he rationalized, had to watch out for her in this mob of people, however much they might love both her and her baby.

She ushered him toward two older women sitting in folding lawn chairs where they could keep an eye on the activities. One was busily engaged in something that resembled crocheting—with kite string.

Loretta bent to kiss their cheeks. "Mama...*Tía* Louisa...I'd like you to meet my employer, Griffin Jones. My car broke down this morning, and he volunteered to bring me to the picnic."

The younger of the two women extended her hand; the other one kept her needle flying. Tatting, Griffin realized.

"Happy birthday, Mrs. Santana," he said, shaking hands with the heavyset woman. Her dark hair was streaked with gray, her flashing eyes sharp with suspicion.

"It's nice you brought Loretta today," her mother said, "but I gotta tell you, it's not right that she's living with you, you two not being married and all."

"I'm his butler, Mama. It's perfectly usual for a butler to live in."

"She's a good girl," she insisted, still speaking to Griffin.

"Yes, ma'am. I know that."

"Mama, please," Loretta pleaded. "You're embarrassing Mr. Jones."

"Call me Griffin, please."

"You oughta be at home with your mama, Lori, the condition you're in. Who's to take care of you, living with a stranger?"

Ignoring the conversation, *Tía* Louisa kept on tatting.

"There's no room at home, Mama. You know that."

"So what's gonna happen when the baby comes? Have you thought about that?"

Griffin hadn't. But he should. If Loretta couldn't go home from the hospital with her baby, where would she go? Soon Rodgers would be back...

"Everything will work out, Mama. You'll see."

Mama didn't seem convinced. "You tell Roberto about your car. He'll fix it for you."

"I will, Mama. As soon as I get a chance."

"I'll see to it her car is repaired," Griffin said. And this time he planned to have the work done by someone who was competent. Loretta needed reliable transportation. For that matter, she just plain needed a new car.

Her mother's eyes narrowed on him. "Anything bad happens to my baby, you'll have to answer to me. You understand that, mister?"

"Yes, ma'am." He began to sweat like an adolescent on a prom date. Any minute now he expected to be told to have Loretta home by midnight or Mama would call the cops.

"Go, then." She waved them away. "Eat. Have fun. Just be sure you get her home early. In her condition, she needs her rest."

Griffin stifled a laugh. "That's exactly what I've been telling her, Mrs. Santana. But she doesn't listen very well, does she?"

Her mother's lips twitched with the threat of a smile. "Maybe she'll learn to listen better to you than she does to her mama."

"I'm working on it." He gave her a conspiratorial smile.

"Maybe I should be encouraging you, eh? Handsome boy like you, and you got money, too."

"Mama!" Tucking her arm through his again, Loretta practically dragged Griffin away from her mother.

"I can't believe what you just did. Do you charm all the women you meet?"

"Most of them," he conceded. "It's a knack I have."

She punched him on the shoulder.

"Ouch." He feigned injury. "I didn't make much of a hit with your aunt Louisa. She didn't say one word."

"That's because she's *deaf.*"

He laughed. "What a relief. I thought I might be losing my touch. I'm usually pretty popular with women over sixty and under fifteen."

"And all those in between, would be my guess."

They halted near the table piled high with desserts, the scent of chocolate mixing with the smell of freshly mowed grass in the cool air. On the soccer field, the players were shouting orders to pass the ball in their direction. The baby in the playpen was still fussing. But Griffin stood with Loretta in an island of quiet, her hand still on his arm, warm and soft, her lilac scent surrounding him. Enticing. Tempting. With the aroma of food in the air and her belly swollen with child, she was both alluring and totally domestic. A disorienting juxtaposition of everything a woman should be.

"Are you hungry yet?" she asked.

For things he couldn't begin to name.

"Our picnics provide a full monthly allowance of cholesterol all in one sitting."

"Then the food ought to be great."

"Yes."

He focused on her lips, remembering how they had felt against his during their one brief encounter. How sweet they had tasted. How hers was the flavor he wanted to savor again.

Something large, round and not in the least soft bashed him on the back of the head. Grunting, he staggered into Loretta, forced to hold on to her so he wouldn't knock her down. Her breasts and belly pressed against him.

Marco came running up to claim the soccer ball that had hit Griffin. "Sorry about that. One of the kids got carried away with his goal kick."

"His aim was a little off, too."

"You got that right. Come on, join in the game," Marco offered. Despite his size and intimidating tattoos, his smile was friendly. "You can be on my team. It's us old guys against the kids, and they've got us outnumbered."

"I'm not exactly up on soccer. Sorry."

"Oh, come on." Marco hooked his arm around Griffin's shoulder like he was one of the family. "Think of this as a training league. Anything goes. And anybody who can learn to toss pizza crusts like you did has got to have great coordination. You'll be fine."

Trying to catch her breath, Loretta watched Griffin being lured into the soccer game. She knew exactly who had kicked the ball at Griffin with complete accuracy. *Rudy,* her former boyfriend, the one who thought she was "used goods." He was out there on the field, looking at her, his lips curled with disapproval. He lived near the park, but she hadn't thought he'd be here or be joining in the family activities.

She wanted to call Griffin back, to warn him Rudy wouldn't play fair. But he was already into the game. From the way he moved agilely around the field, he'd be able to hold his own, even if he didn't know much about soccer.

Still, she wished he'd stayed with her. And she had no right to wish for any such thing.

Griffin lost track of Loretta while he was playing soccer, but when the men decided to take a break for lunch, she found him. They filled their plates to overflowing and ate sitting on the ground with their backs to a tree, family members ebbing and flowing around them, visiting with Loretta, eyeing Griffin with open curiosity. Their interest didn't make him particularly uncomfortable. More than anything they simply seemed concerned about her and her health. And he was a stranger in their midst.

Maybe he'd misjudged her family. They certainly seemed as loving as any he'd ever met—not that he was an expert.

After a while Marco prodded him back into the soccer game. Since Loretta was content where she was, Griffin agreed to give it one more try, then they'd head for home.

He didn't last long this time. Given a full stomach, he was no match for the younger players. He went in search of Loretta.

When he couldn't spot her, Griffin asked her mother.

"Maybe she went to the ladies'," she said. "When a girl's pregnant like that, she's gotta go a lot."

"Right. I'll check." He hadn't given much thought to the physical symptoms of being pregnant, and Loretta never complained, at least not around him. He wondered if she really didn't mind the discomfort, or if in her delicate body she had a courageous heart. From what he knew of Loretta, he suspected the latter.

The rest room was a squat concrete building with a tile roof and wire mesh covering the high windows. He hung around a minute near the women's side but no one came or went, and there was no sign of Loretta. He glanced back toward the picnic area, still unable to spot her.

A shimmer of apprehension traveled along his spine. What if she...

Then he heard a sobbing sound coming from the bathroom.

"Loretta? Are you in there?"

No answer.

"Loretta! If you're in there—"

She appeared at the doorway, her eyes red-rimmed, a damp tissue in her hand.

Panic clutched at him and he dashed toward her. "Lori?" he said in haste, her family nickname an intimacy that came easily to him. "Are you all right? What's wrong? Is it the baby?"

Shaking her head, she blew her nose.

Bending, he looked into her tear-streaked face. "What happened?" he asked gently. If someone had hurt her, he'd kill him with his bare hands.

"Noth...ing." She sniffed and her voice caught.

"Right. You were just in there having a good cry all by yourself?"

She nodded, looking at him with soulful, sad eyes. "It's just my hormones. That's all."

He didn't believe her. "Honey, tell me what's wrong."

She blinked and hiccuped. "It was...Rudy."

Rudy—the man she'd been dating. If he'd so much as *touched* Loretta, the guy was a dead man. "What'd he do?"

"Nothing, really. He just said some awful, hurtful things. He didn't used to be so mean."

Relief eased the tight grip he had on himself. "What did he say, sweetheart?"

"That I'm getting stuck-up and snooty…and acting better than I am. That I'm fat and ugly and no different than a…" Tears spilled from her eyes. "Because I'm having somebody else's baby. He says nobody…nobody's ever going to want to marry me."

Sick at heart for Loretta and furious at the jerk who had called her names, Griffin wrapped her in his arms. He held her close as she cried, her tears soaking through his shirt. Instinctively he brushed a kiss to the top of her head, her hair like satin.

"It's a lie, sweetheart. Everything that jerk said is a lie."

"I know, but he c-called me a tramp," she said, her voice wobbling. "Why would he d-do that when he knows I've never, ever m-made love with anyone?"

Closing his eyes against the intense pain of her emotion, he held her tight. *A virgin.* And she'd agreed to have another woman's baby. Without knowing the pleasure of making love she was risking her life for the child she was carrying.

He caressed her head, smoothing her hair, and felt the fullness of her figure nestled against his body. "You're the most loving, caring woman I've ever known. Hundreds of guys are going to want to marry you. You'll see."

She hiccuped again and drew a shaky breath.

"I'm sorry. I don't usually take things so personally."

He lifted her chin. "You're beautiful, Lori. If anyone tells you different, they're lying or just plain jealous. You radiate beauty from the inside out. Your pregnancy makes you even more lovely. More womanly."

"That's the nicest thing..."

"I mean it." It was the most natural thing in the world for Griffin to kiss her then. In some ways he meant the kiss to be medicinal, to cure the damage Rudy had done to her self-esteem. But the kiss was more than that.

He cupped her cheek, feeling the elemental flow of her feminine power overtake him. He tasted salt on her lips, sweetness in her breath, surrender as she leaned into him. He deepened the intimacy of their kiss, tasting her more fully.

Her hand circled his neck, her slender fingers threading through the hair at his nape as she tentatively touched the tip of her tongue to his. A low moan escaped her lips; a tremor of response shook Griffin. She wanted him in the same way he wanted her.

That appalling thought brought him up short. She was virtually nine months pregnant! And a virgin. He'd be a fiend to try to take her now, in her condition, here behind an ugly rest room in a city park. And that's exactly what his body wanted him to do. His good reason said otherwise.

Guilt assailed him. He eased his embrace and broke the kiss. Her lips were damp, her eyes wide, her breath coming in little pants. His own heart was hammering like a computer keyboard set on high-speed automatic.

Dammit, what had he been thinking of?

"I'm sorry, Loretta. I shouldn't have—"

"Don't apologize. You were only trying to be nice."

"I guess I got a little carried away." Using the pad of his thumb, he brushed residual tears from her cheek, so soft it was like caressing a downy feather. "I came looking for you, figuring it was time to go home."

"Yes. Home." Loretta slid her gaze away from the man who had just kissed her, the man who Rudy had accused her of trying to trap into marriage. He'd called her hoity-toity, saying she was trying to land a rich husband when she was no better than a tramp.

Rudy didn't understand. It wasn't that she didn't like Griffin, or that she couldn't imagine herself falling in love with him. What woman wouldn't?

But more than anyone else, Loretta knew she'd never measure up to a man like Griffin. His wealth, his smooth charm, were all too much for her. This wasn't a storybook, and her name wasn't Cinderella.

All the more reason why she would cherish each day she was allowed to remain in his employ.

She swallowed the rest of her tears as they walked toward his car, carols playing from a distant radio. Being a butler wasn't all that bad. Not when your boss was Griffin Jones.

She just wished he hadn't apologized for kissing her, because in her heart she wanted him to do it again.

Chapter Eight

Her hormones were definitely on the fritz.

Since yesterday, when Griffin had kissed her, Loretta's mind had been traveling down erotic paths at the least little encouragement. Even the rainfall that had started during the night hadn't managed to douse her fevered imagination.

She remembered in exquisite detail how he had held her, gently caressing her, the warmth of his lips on hers. She'd never before been kissed like that, so totally possessed by a man, so totally giving of herself. Wanting to hold nothing back. The rest of the world had ceased to exist. Only she and Griffin remained, cocooned in a sensual universe of his making.

Shaking the rain off her umbrella, she stepped into the headquarters of Compuworks, Griffin's uncle Matt's company. Maybe on the way home she'd stop by a health food store. Surely they'd have something to calm her wayward thoughts—the urges that had kept her tossing and turning all night. The dull ache in her back reminded her just how little sleep she'd managed.

Umbrella in hand, she approached the pretty, young receptionist at the front desk. "I'd like to see Mr. Matt Jones. Would you please tell him Griffin Jones's butler is here and it's quite urgent I speak with him."

As the young woman reached for the phone, she gave Loretta a puzzled frown. Minutes later she was still looking confused when she buzzed Loretta through the security door to the executive offices.

Unlike his nephew, Mathew Jones wasn't a particularly handsome man. Tall and slender, he was almost angular, his features too sharp to be described as good-looking. But his blue eyes were kind, his smile welcoming, as he led Loretta to an upholstered chair in the corner of his modest office. Immediately she felt right at home, almost as if she was visiting family.

Only a few miles away, Ralph entered Griffin's office without knocking. "Jonesy, we've got ourselves two problems."

Griffin rubbed his eyes with the heels of his hands. He hadn't slept well last night. Too much food at the picnic, he told himself. *Or too many kisses.* "Great. I thought we had a whole lot more than two problems." Not the least of which were his confused feelings about Loretta—*a pregnant virgin.*

"Yeah, but these are just the two immediate ones."

He leaned back in his chair, the springs creaking. "So give me the bad news."

"The train that was carrying about a million bucks worth of our computers and peripherals from the factory in Baja went off the track. Apparently the rain had softened the railroad bed just enough that it gave way."

"How long will it take them to repair the track?"

"Long enough that if we wait we won't have enough time to get the computers into the warehouse and then distributed to our stores before the ad hits the paper this weekend."

"Swell." He shoved back from his desk and stood, plowing his fingers through his hair. Outside, the rain was no more than a light drizzle but enough to derail a train and maybe keep a few customers away. In a tight market with only days left until Christmas, this was not the kind of problem he needed. "What do you propose we do?"

Ralph sat down in the chair in front of the desk, stretching his legs out and crossing his ankles. "I'm not sure. Our trucks are already on the road making deliveries. I guess we'll have to rent trucks, get a moving company or somebody to pick up the merchandise. Maybe send out the warehouse people with them. It's gonna cost us, and that's assuming the computers aren't busted."

Another expense he didn't need. Damn it all! His father had died believing Griffin would make a success of Compuware, make it grow. He didn't want to betray his father's trust; he didn't want to fail. "I guess we don't have much of a choice."

"I'll see what kind of deal I can work—"

A knock on the door interrupted Ralph.

"Hello." Loretta stuck her head in the office, smiling. "Your secretary isn't at her desk. Are you busy?"

Griffin straightened, surprised to see Loretta at his door, particularly in her butler uniform. He'd left the house before she got up that morning, not sure he wanted to face her over the breakfast table after their kiss in the park. "A little. We just heard a train went off the track with a load of our computers onboard."

Her expression turned troubled. "Oh, I heard about that on the news, but I didn't know your company had anything on the train. What are you going to do?" She glanced from Griffin to Ralph, who'd stood when she entered the office. Griffin made brief introductions.

"We're going to rent trucks to pick up the computers," Ralph told her.

"You don't have to do that," she said.

Griffin frowned. "We need the merchandise in the stores and can't wait—"

"I mean you don't have to *rent* them. Roberto has a half-dozen rentals at his garage. It's part of his business. He'll loan them to you."

A bad feeling knotted Griffin's stomach. "That's

okay. We've already decided to use a regular moving company.''

"Don't be silly." She crossed the room and picked up the phone on Griffin's desk. "Why should you spend your good money when Roberto would be happy to help you out?''

"The last time he *helped* me, it cost me a fortune to have my car repainted—forget the tune-up he botched.''

She punched in Roberto's phone number. "Oh, that was simply a misunderstanding. Somebody was pulling his leg when they told him your car was green, and of course he can't— Hi, Roberto, it's Loretta. I need a favor for Griffin...''

In mute astonishment, Griffin listened as Loretta arranged for trucks and drivers—all of them cousins, it sounded like—to drop whatever they were doing and head for San Diego to the train wreck, pick up the computers and return the merchandise to Compuware's warehouse in L.A. She was like a general maneuvering her troops. Given his history with Roberto, Griffin wasn't sure if he'd be considered an ally or an enemy.

"There, we're all set," she said, hanging up the phone. She beamed Griffin a smile.

"How much is all of this going to cost me?'' Griffin asked, suspicious of the whole deal. Loretta's brother wasn't exactly the most reliable auto mechanic in the world. Hard to believe his U-Hauls would be in very good shape.

"Nothing. Well, you could pay Roberto for his

gas, if you'd like but he's doing this as a favor to me. You know, we're family."

That didn't make a whole lot of sense to Griffin since he wasn't part of the Santana clan. Besides, in his experience, families didn't work that way.

But the arrangements Loretta had made *sounded* solid. If he could trust Roberto.

"Ralph, why don't you take a couple of our guys and get over to Roberto's. If everything looks okay—"

"It's all arranged," Loretta insisted. "Roberto is happy to help you out. He says to tell you, with a little more practice you'll be a great soccer player— for an old guy." She giggled.

Eyeing Griffin curiously, Ralph said, "I'll take care of it, boss."

At least Griffin could trust Brainerd's judgment. If the trucks weren't up to snuff or the cousins were incompetent, Ralph would tell 'em no deal.

"I'll let you two get back to work," Loretta said. "I just wanted to make sure you'd be home for dinner on Thursday night." Expectantly she looked at Griffin.

"I guess. Why?"

"Oh, I'm planning something special," she said with a shrug. "I wanted to be sure that'd be a good night for you. That you didn't have a date or anything like that."

"I'll be home." For the past couple of weeks, he'd either been on the road or at home with Loretta during the evening hours. Now that he thought of it, his social life had pretty well dried up. Oddly he hadn't missed it. He supposed he'd been too busy with business problems to give it much thought. And going to family picnics. But he had to hope she hadn't come up with a new recipe for tofu and broccoli.

"I'll see you later, then." With a jaunty wave of her hand, Loretta left.

Ralph started to follow her.

"Wait a minute, Brainerd. You said earlier we had two problems. What's number two?"

Ralph stopped by the door, then came back inside, closing it behind him. "I don't think you're going to like this, boss."

He hadn't liked the first problem. How much worse could it be than having merchandise stranded on a train track? "Tell me, anyway."

"I was driving down Venice Boulevard this morning on the way to work. I went right past Compuworks's headquarters."

Griffin waited for a second shoe to drop. "And?"

"I saw your butler going inside."

"Into Compuworks?"

"You got it."

He didn't like the sound of this. "How did you know it was Loretta?"

"Come on, Jonesy. How many pregnant women do you know who drive a beat-up Datsun like the one you drove to the office a couple of weeks ago and walk around in a black maternity tux? And now that I've met her..."

Griffin sat down heavily in his chair. Why would Loretta visit Uncle Matt's company? Particularly when she knew there'd been a breach between the two firms for years? It didn't make any sense....

Shoving his hands in his pockets, Ralph rattled some coins together. "Compuworks's prices matched up dollar for dollar with ours on the last ad. I hate to suggest it, but would Loretta have access to that kind of information at your place?"

She would. Griffin often worked at home, and his computer there was linked to the office. Loretta, it turned out, knew more about computers than she had initially let on. But if she were trying to undermine his company—if she was spying for Uncle Matt— why had she been so helpful when she discovered his employees weren't providing adequate customer service?

It didn't make sense. And he didn't like the thought that Loretta was anything but what she had professed to be—a pregnant woman who needed a job.

"I'll look into it, Brainy. You see if you can get that shipment of computers up here in one piece."

Loretta had the whole-grain spaghetti casserole heating in the oven when the phone rang.

"Good evening, Jones residence. This is the butler speaking." Cocking her shoulder, she held the phone to her ear while she wiped her hands on a tea towel.

"Is that you, Miss Santana?"

"Oh, hi, Rodgers." She'd recognize his refined British accent anywhere. "How's your mother?"

"Getting on a bit better these days, according to the doctor."

"I'm glad to hear that."

He paused a moment on the other end of the line. "I must say, I'm a bit surprised you're still in Mr. Jones's employ."

"Oh, we've been getting on splendidly. And I'll have you know, I haven't once had to use my typing skills."

"No, miss, I imagine not."

"So, are you planning to come back soon?"

"I should think I'll be able to return in about a week, a day or two before Christmas, I imagine. If you'd pass that information on to young Mr. Jones, I'd be most grateful."

"Sure." She did a few quick calculations. If she was able to keep working for another full week, she'd be eligible for insurance coverage—just. "There's no rush for you to hurry home. Stay and enjoy the holidays with your mother. I've got everything under control here."

"Actually, miss, Mum has had an amazing recovery and I'm finding her a bit of a nag. As well, the damp weather here is no longer to my taste. Bad joints, you know."

"Well, gosh, Rodgers, it's raining here, too. Bucketfuls. Maybe you ought to stop off somewhere warm and dry on your way back. I've heard the Caribbean is a great place to spend Christmas."

"No doubt the rain will cease before I return."

She smiled weakly. "No doubt. And I'm sure Mr. Jones will be happy to have you back whenever you decide to return." And Loretta didn't imagine she'd be within her rights to bar the door to Rodgers just so she could work an extra day or two to earn her insurance coverage.

After Rodgers bid her a good-evening and hung up, Loretta held the phone in her hand, thinking. Whatever was she going to do if Rodgers came back too soon? She couldn't afford a hospital without insurance and didn't want to take charity from her family.

For that matter, she didn't know what she'd do after the baby was born.

Her cousin Brenna had offered her a place and had even been willing to give Loretta the boys' room while they slept on a glass-enclosed porch. But Loretta had insisted she and the baby should take the porch rather than disrupt the household so much, and in lieu of paying rent, she volunteered to serve as a live-in nanny for Brian and Cody.

The truth was she would much rather have her own apartment. But without a job, that wasn't possible.

Cradling the phone, she leaned her forehead against the cupboard. Her eyes burned with tears she refused to shed. Everyone knew women got emotional when they were pregnant. No reason for her to be any different.

Her throat convulsed as she swallowed a sob.

How much nicer it would be if she and her baby had a real room to share—something like Rodgers's room would be a true luxury, warm and cozy. She could curtain off a tiny corner for the baby. That would be all they'd need.

But she had dreamed of more.

She'd stood at the doorway of one of the upstairs bedrooms in Griffin's house imagining it as a nursery. She saw the room decorated with cute wallpaper, a musical teddy bear mobile hanging above a white crib with matching sheets. In the matching dresser the drawers were filled with dainty sleepers and in the closet there were frilly dresses Mari would love to wear.

But only in the most secret part of her heart had she dreamed that while her baby slept securely in that upstairs room, that she—Loretta—would be sleeping in the adjacent room. In Griffin's arms.

No, she didn't dare admit that dream, not even to herself. Because shattered dreams could break a woman's heart.

It was well past dinnertime when Griffin finally got home. In addition to waiting for word from Brainerd and leaving late from the office, there'd been a couple of fender benders on the rain-slicked canyon road that slowed traffic to a stop. He'd heard on the radio that northern California was getting drenched with this early season storm. In L.A. it only took a few drops of rain to cause havoc on the streets. He hated to think what would happen if it rained here as hard as it was coming down up north. More than once since he'd owned the house, the Topanga Canyon creek had overflowed its banks, creating all kinds of problems in the neighborhood, including landslides that cut them off from the highway for days at a time.

He entered the house through the garage door and followed the sound of the TV playing.

In the family room, Loretta was sitting on the floor propped up by a bunch of pillows, panting, and watching the Lamaze tape. She was wearing shorts, and her sleeveless top stretched tightly over her belly. His gut clenched. She'd be having her baby anyday now. What if something went wrong? God help him, what if she died the way his mother had?

Dammit! Why wasn't she with her family where *they'd* be responsible for her, not Griffin?

She looked up from her practice session, her cheeks flushed. "Hi. Did you get things straightened out at the train wreck?"

"Our merchandise is all in the warehouse where it belongs. Roberto and his crew did a good job." Much to Griffin's surprise.

"I told you it'd be okay." She grinned at him. "Your dinner's keeping warm in the oven."

"I'll get it in a minute." He'd meant to confront her about being at his uncle Matt's but he didn't want to do anything that would upset her, nothing that could bring on premature labor. "I thought you were going to get one of your relatives to help you with that Lamaze business."

"Oh, they'll know what to do when the time comes." She shifted her position on the floor, looking uncomfortable, and wiped sweat from her brow. "It's me that has a problem. I've got the breathing down pretty well but I can't seem to do the relaxing part right."

"What do you mean?"

"On the tape, her husband...the coach...rubs her back and does all these really nice things to relax her. Alone, I can't..." Her chin quivered. She forced a smile, her eyes glistening. "Guess that comes from not having a husband."

Ah, hell...

Tossing his jacket on a chair, he knelt beside her. No matter his intentions, he kept being drawn into playing a role he didn't want. Being responsible for her. Pretending to be her husband. Even being involved with her family. But dammit, she needed help and he was here. How could he turn his back on her? How could he, even for a minute, think she was a spy for Uncle Matt's company?

"Show me what needs to be done," he said.

"You don't have to—"

"Somebody does, and I don't exactly see anybody else stepping forward. Think of me as your substitute coach." But not as her husband. He'd been a playboy most of his life. That was *safe,* a role he knew how to play. Just like his father had, after Griffin's mother died. He'd always had a beautiful woman on his arm, but none who Griffin had thought worthy of replacing his mother.

Using the remote, she rolled the tape back to the beginning. He helped her to her feet and she sat on the chair where she could see the TV while he pulled up the footstool in front of her. In a cheerful voice, the narrator provided relaxation instructions.

"All right, coaches, we want our mommies to be all relaxed, from the top of their heads clear down to their toes."

Sitting so close to Loretta, where he could look into the depths of her velvety eyes, Griffin didn't feel in the least relaxed.

Following the instructions, his knees placed on either side of hers, he slid his fingers into her hair, the strands like a skein of black silk. He massaged her scalp. The sweet floral scent of her wafted around him.

She licked her lips, and he felt the motion right where her knees touched his thighs.

"Rodgers called today. His mother seems to be improving."

"That's good." Griffin circled her temples with the pads of his thumbs.

"He'll probably come home in a week or so."

He kneaded the tension from the back of her neck and stroked her shoulders. Her skin was as soft as a baby's, fragrant with lilacs and womanhood. "That means he'll be here before the baby comes."

"Yes, the timing's perfect."

"Where will you go?"

Swallowing hard, her eyelids fluttered closed.

"My cousin Brenna says I can come stay with them. I'll help take care of her boys."

He rotated her shoulders, loose and relaxed. A crucial part of his anatomy was anything but slack. "Those two kids who spent the night here?"

"Yes." She breathed out the word.

The narrator urged him to use steady, slow movements. Firm hands. Long, easy strokes. *Slow hands,* like making love.

"You're going to have your hands full with the baby pretty soon. You don't need a rambunctious pair of hellions on your hands, too."

"They're good boys."

If Loretta could read his thoughts, she'd know he wasn't thinking like a boy at all. Definitely a full-grown man. And his thoughts were inappropriate as hell.

She opened her eyes. "The baby's moving. I think she wants to say hello." Taking his hand, she placed it on her belly. The baby moved.

"She's getting stronger," he said, his eyes on Loretta.

"I already love her so much. I can hardly wait to hold her."

But who would be holding Loretta, he wondered. Who would be there when she needed a good cry because someone had hurt her feelings? It wasn't fair she had to carry so many burdens alone.

He gritted his teeth. *Not my problem.*

Holding his hand to her belly, Loretta felt the connection between him, her baby and herself, only lay-

ers of fabric and flesh separating them. It took only
the tiniest stretch of her imagination to think of this
man with his flashing, silver-blue eyes as her husband, the father of her child. To pretend for an instant that he loved her and she loved him.

A lock of his tobacco-brown hair had slipped
down. If they were lovers, she'd have the right to
smooth it back from his forehead. To lean forward
and place a kiss on his lips. To tell him about her
fears.

But they were not lovers; he wasn't her husband.

However much she might like it to be so, that
could never happen. A millionaire playboy and her?
The thought was laughable, though in truth she felt
more like crying.

"Griffin?" She whispered his name, hoarse and
thick in her throat.

The baby moved again, restless.

"Yeah?"

"The tape... It ended."

He blinked. Slowly he lifted his hand and slid
back away from her.

Outside, the rain dripped from the eaves, a rhyth-
mic plinking of drops on the redwood decking beyond the French doors. In the distance a siren wailed
and was answered by the closer call of a coyote.

Loretta shivered. Never had she felt so alone, or
so afraid, not since her mother abandoned her in that
dark, dreary motel.

Chapter Nine

"Thank goodness you're home on time." Loretta hustled Griffin into the house Thursday evening, practically snatching his raincoat and jacket off his back and handing him a pullover cashmere sweater before he could get his bearings. "You'll be more comfortable if you're dressed casually."

"I will?" Tired from a long day at the office, he peered past her into the dining room. In the center of the table, festive red candles were arranged in a holiday display of pinecones and greenery. The overhead lights were dimmed and there were wine-glasses at the two places. "What's going on?"

"I told you I was planning something special for tonight."

His spirits perked up, and he smiled. "Looks like an intimate dinner for two. Who am I having dinner with?" Eyeing Loretta and the bright red bow tie she'd substituted for her usual black one, he decided she'd do just fine for a dinner partner. He could only hope she wasn't trying out a new tofu recipe that would spoil their evening's private celebration.

"You'll see, and I know you'll be pleased." She urged him toward the living room where a cheerful fire crackled in the fireplace and dime-store decorations brightened the oak mantel.

"You've been busy," he commented. Most years he didn't decorate his house for the holidays, opting instead to invite a current girlfriend out on the town. This was kind of nice—sort of homey. Though she shouldn't be spending her hard-earned money on stuff for his place, and he'd make sure she got reimbursed.

"Christmas is my favorite time of the year. Especially when families get together. I thought a few decorations would put you in a holiday mood for this evening."

"All I need to make the picture perfect are my slippers and a pipe."

She looked at him blankly. "You don't smoke a pipe. Besides, secondary smoke would be bad for the baby."

He swallowed a smile. "You're right. I'll just stick with the slippers."

"I'll have to go upstairs—"

"I'm only teasing, Lori. Relax." He didn't want her running up and down the stairs fetching him things. She ought to be—

"Now you just sit yourself down," she ordered.

"Enjoy the fire. Rest a little, and I'll see to the dinner."

Before he could object, she'd hurried from the room. Waddled, actually. Her pregnancy was so far along, it was a wonder she could walk at all. Griffin worried about that. They were a good half hour from the hospital, longer if it was raining—which it had been all day.

What was she up to, he wondered. Why was tonight so special?

Maybe she was planning to leave. They'd have a quiet dinner together, she'd tell him she was moving back in with her relatives, and that would be that. He wouldn't have to worry about getting her to a hospital or anywhere else.

His insides twisted into a knot, and he leaned an elbow on the fireplace mantel, staring into the fire. Somehow after the past few weeks, *not* worrying about Loretta seemed unnatural. He would at least want to make sure she and her baby were both okay. Maybe send a gift after the baby was born.

Before she left, he told himself, he'd get her forwarding address and ask that she have somebody give him a call when the baby came.

Sweat broke out on his forehead. *Women died in childbirth.*

The doorbell rang, and he started, feeling an instant of relief.

Maybe tonight wasn't Loretta's last night at all, he thought with a grin. Maybe to make amends for all the trouble she'd caused on her first night here,

Loretta had invited Aileen over for an intimate dinner for two. That would be just like his butler—worrying about him instead of taking care of herself.

Problem was, he wasn't interested in Aileen anymore.

Turning away from the fireplace, he headed for the door. Automatically, he straightened his tie and ran a hand through his hair.

Loretta scurried past him at full waddle. Breathlessly she said, "I'll get it. You wait right there."

Amused, he waited in the middle of the living room as instructed. He hadn't thought about Aileen since his pizza-making adventure with Loretta. To his surprise a raven-haired pregnant woman had managed to replace all memory of his urge to date a beautiful redhead. He probably should have called...

He heard a man's voice in the entryway and Loretta's reply. A shiver of unease prickled the back of his neck. What man would be—

Loretta popped into the room, a black umbrella dripping water on the carpet in her hand, a man's raincoat draped over her arm. She smiled with a forced brightness. "Look who's come to see you."

Shock, as if he'd taken a punch to the gut, drove the air from Griffin's lungs.

Uncle Matt. Grayer than when Griffin had last seen him, thinner and slightly stooped. Ten years older.

The bile of betrayal rose in Griffin's throat. He

shot Loretta an accusing look. "You did this. You invited him here when you knew—"

"I should have made the effort to reconcile with you years ago," his uncle said calmly. "It took this remarkable young woman to remind me about the importance of family."

Griffin snorted derisively as Loretta slipped out of sight down the hallway. "She would. And all it took was one little reminder from her, and now we're supposed to be a lovey-dovey family? I don't think so, Uncle Matt. Not after what you did to my father."

Unhurried, Uncle Matt strolled into the room, walking to the fireplace. He held out his hands to warm them. "What is it you think I did to Everett?" he asked without turning around.

Griffin closed his eyes. "Dammit! I don't know. My father wouldn't tell me. He said he didn't want to disillusion me about my *favorite* uncle."

A shudder shook Matt's shoulders. "Perhaps it's time then that you heard the truth."

Griffin didn't want to. It was a lose-lose situation. He could forever and always lose the uncle he remembered so fondly. Or he could lose the respect he'd felt for his father. Either way, Griffin would have to surrender beliefs that had been a powerful part of his life—beliefs that had made him strong.

Studying the man standing at the fireplace, a frail imitation of what he'd been ten years ago, Griffin could almost hear Loretta admonishing him, *He's family. Give him a chance.* His shoulders slumped in defeat.

"I'll listen, Uncle Matt."

Raising his head and turning, Matt smiled. "You have the look of your father, his way about you. A handsome lady-killer, would be my guess. I wasn't so equally blessed as you and my brother."

Griffin had no idea where this story was going. Sure, he knew his dad had run around—*after* his wife had died. While it might not have made him an angel, it sure as hell hadn't made him a devil, either.

"My wife and I had a good marriage. We'd raised two children together. But Everett was capable of turning any woman's head, if he put his mind to it."

Griffin felt the bottom drop out of his stomach. "Are you telling me my father and Aunt Margaret had an affair?"

"She was very flattered by his attention. What woman wouldn't be? But when I found out—"

Griffin swore, low and succinctly. He didn't have to listen to his uncle slander his father. His dad wouldn't do that, not hit on that old persimmon of a woman, so dried-up that she—

But maybe she hadn't been quite so dried-up then. Or maybe his father, who'd worn his lady-killer image as a badge of honor, had viewed her as a challenge. Some kind of crazy sibling rivalry bone he'd wanted to win.

He sat heavily on the couch. "Don't lie to me, Uncle Matt."

"I won't, son. Your aunt Margaret and I have long since reconciled our differences. In some ways, it made our marriage stronger. Now I'd just like to reconcile with you. We are, as your young lady says with a great deal of passion, *family*."

In the kitchen Loretta held her breath waiting for the sound of shouting—or breaking glass. She desperately wanted Griffin and his uncle to reestablish the family linkage. She sensed in both men a deep loneliness.

Family, she knew, could fill that terrible void.

As the minutes ticked by in gratifying silence, she checked on the meat and turned down the oven to keep their dinner warm. Outside the rain dripped from the eaves, and the windows steamed against the cool air.

Finally Griffin shoved open the kitchen door. His features looked strained and weary.

"Are you mad at me?" she asked in a whisper.

Shaking his head, he smiled wryly. "No, if anything I'm grateful. But if you don't serve dinner pretty soon, you'll have a couple of hungry bears on your hands. Our stomachs are both growling."

She exhaled in relief, her spirits lifting like a cloud after a passing storm. "Two minutes and dinner will be on the table."

Candlelight flickered across Griffin's face, the flames reflecting in his eyes like tiny beacons. For a moment Loretta imagined she was alone with him at a fancy restaurant enjoying a romantic evening for two. Then Matt's laughter drew her back into the story Griffin was telling.

"We went on this god-awful camping trip. Remember that, Uncle Matt? I don't think either you or Dad had a clue how to start a campfire, much less cook anything over it. And the mosquitoes were this big." Griffin held his hands a foot apart. "But you two thought us kids ought to know how to catch a fish. Some ridiculous rite of passage. Finally we packed up the tent, sleeping bags and all, and headed for the nearest motel. We kids played pinball half the night at the coffee shop next door. It was great."

Leaning back in her chair, Loretta smiled as she listened to the two men reminiscing. They'd insisted she join them at the dinner table for dessert, though she'd told them she'd already eaten. Which really wasn't true.

She'd had little appetite all day, her back aching so badly she'd barely made it through dinner preparations. Though she was glad Griffin and his uncle were getting along so well together, she really wished they'd finish their desserts and leave. Both of them.

The ache intensified and she pressed her lips together. There were still dishes to do, the kitchen to clean up.

"If you'll excuse me, gentlemen." She rose from her chair. "I've got to earn my keep."

"And I must go," Matt said, glancing at his watch. "It's later than I had realized."

"I'll come help you with the cleanup in a minute," Griffin promised Loretta. "I'll just see Uncle Matt out first."

"No rush," she mumbled, her teeth hurting with the pain that scourged her back.

She carried the dessert plates into the kitchen, rinsed them and put them in the dishwasher. The pan she'd roasted the leg of lamb in was still on the stove, burned drippings coagulated in the bottom, and she needed to slice the remainder of the meat to use for leftovers. The braised potatoes—

She groaned as another pain tightened in her lower back. Clinging to the edge of the tile counter, her knuckles turned white. "No," she whispered, "please, not till the insurance..."

Griffin burst back into the kitchen. "I've got to thank you, Loretta. I was a fool not to get a hold of Uncle Matt after Dad died." He slid his arm around her waist and planted a kiss on her cheek. "He's a pretty terrific guy, isn't he?"

"Yes." She straightened as the pain eased. Only her imagination, she told herself. *Days* too early for labor to begin. She'd simply been on her feet too much today.

Griffin picked up a dinner plate and scraped the bits of food into the sink. "Uncle Matt and I talked about merging our two companies again. He wants to retire, and his kids aren't interested in the business. His oldest boy is a doctor—a plastic surgeon. And the other kid is studying journalism. He's planning to win a Pulitzer prize or something."

Feeling a little dizzy, Loretta moved out of the way to let Griffin finish. Lots of women had false labor before the real thing happens. The pain would stop in a little bit, then she'd feel foolish to have worried at all.

"Of course, there'd be a lot of details to iron out. Who'd have controlling interest—which stores, if any, would close, that sort of thing."

She tried to concentrate on Griffin's excitement and the business issues. "Compuware and Compuworks would hold a big market share if you merged."

"We'd gain a lot of economies of scale." Finding the scouring pad under the sink, he started to work scrubbing the roasting pan. "By the way, he said Compuworks was beating our prices because he knew what markup we'd be using and so he dropped his by five percent. He was more interested in volume than profit margin."

Her legs wouldn't hold up her any longer. Pulling out a chair at the kitchen table, she sat down. The thrumming in her back reached a crescendo.

Griffin glanced over his shoulder. "Loretta?"

She couldn't answer.

"What's wrong?" He grabbed a towel to dry his hands. "Is it the baby?"

"No. It's too soon."

He knelt beside her, concern in his eyes. "Maybe Mari has other ideas."

"It's three more days until—" she squeezed her eyes shut "—until I'm eligible for insurance."

"Forget the damn insurance."

"I can't. I don't have any money. Not nearly enough to pay for the hospital. It's too early. It's probably false labor, anyway. I'll...I'll just cross my legs."

He didn't look convinced. "From the looks of you, three days is going to be a long time to keep your legs crossed. You better at least let me call the doctor."

She shook her head. "I'll be fine. Just give me a minute or two. You'll see."

Sitting back on his haunches, Griffin figured his worst nightmare was about to come true. All the excitement of reuniting with his uncle had been wiped away, replaced by a terror that coiled through his midsection. Loretta was about to have her baby. *Now.* And he was responsible.

He'd been afraid this might actually happen, so after their Lamaze session he'd gone on the Internet, checking out everything he could find on delivering babies, including all the things that could go wrong. At the moment, however, his mind had gone blank. Paralysis threatened everything except his pounding heart.

He fought against the immobilizing fear. "So how often are your, uh, pains coming?"

"It's not labor." She pressed her thighs together as if that would prevent her baby from popping out.

Sweat crept down Griffin's spine. "Yeah, well...do you have your bag packed?" He'd read that somewhere—on the Internet or maybe he'd seen it in a movie. Guys asked that sort of question of their wives…or maybe girlfriends. But not their *butlers*.

She nodded. "In my bedroom. All I need is my toothbrush and deodorant. But I'm not going to the hospital. Not yet."

"Lori, sweetheart, it's raining cats and dogs outside. It's going to take nearly an hour to get to—"

With a sharp intake of air, she doubled over.

Griffin shot to his feet. "Okay, that's it. No more argument. I don't care about the insurance. I'll pay for your damned hospital expenses. And I'm taking you there right now."

Her big brown eyes filled with tears as deep as the rain puddles outside. "I don't want charity."

"It's a Christmas bonus, okay?" Trying not to reveal how terrified he was for her and the baby— or for himself—he smoothed the fine hairs dampened with sweat back from her forehead. "You wait here, sweetheart. I'll get your bag and we'll be on our way."

His hands sweating, his stomach knotting, Griffin managed to latch her suitcase closed, find Loretta's coat, which he draped over her shoulders, and get her out to the car in the garage. He didn't worry about the rest of the dinner dishes or turning off the lights. He only wanted to get her safely to the hospital where someone else could take charge—could be responsible.

When he backed out of the garage, the rain was like a waterfall, visibility practically nil. He crept down the hill, water sluicing down his driveway toward the raging creek he had to cross in order to get to the highway. His headlights bounced off the rain like it was a sheet of tin. He peered ahead through the storm.

The roar began as a low rumble. Soon the sound rose to a thunderous level. Wood cracked. Metal squealed, tearing bolts loose from their moorings. Debris racing down the overflowing creek slammed into the bridge with explosive force.

"Griffin!" Loretta gasped.

He slowed even further. "Yeah. I see it." The old wooden bridge that spanned what used to be a twenty-foot-wide dry creek bed had broken free on his end. The press of the current shoved it into the middle of the stream. With another ear-splitting roar the bridge slid away from the far shore, beginning a bobbing, slow-motion journey down the flooded stream.

As surely as if they were on an island at the center of a hurricane, they were cut off from escape.

"What are we going to do?" Loretta's voice trembled.

"Go back to the house." He shoved the car into reverse. "The rescue people will get you out of here and safely to a hospital in plenty of time. Don't worry."

His admonishment to not worry sounded damn strange to Griffin's ears. He was scared spitless, fear making it hard for him to draw a breath. But he wanted Loretta to remain calm. To not let her see his own terror would require an acting job worthy of an Oscar nomination.

It had been raining the night his mother died.

He hit the automatic opener and the garage door responded, lifting as he drove the Mercedes back inside. The power was still on. That was a good sign.

He helped Loretta out of the car, ushering her into the house. "You sit here on the couch," he told her as he led her into the family room. "I'll call 911. They'll get someone out here in a hurry."

She grabbed his hand, her eyes wide, her fingers icy cold. "I'm afraid, Griffin. Don't leave me."

"You know I won't let anything bad happen to you, sweetheart. Just let me go call for help, and I'll be right back."

He slid his hand free of hers and hurried into the kitchen.

The emergency operator took forever to answer. "What is the nature of your emergency?"

"I've got a pregnant woman here and she's gone into labor. The rain has washed out the bridge over the creek and we're cut off."

The operator confirmed his address. "There've been several mud slides along Topanga Canyon, sir. We may have some difficulty—"

"Look, this is a real emergency. She's gonna have her baby—"

"I understand, sir. The road is washed out—"

"Can't you send a helicopter or something?" In this weather? He must be crazy.

"We'll do everything we—"

The line went dead. Not just the operator hanging up but the whole system had gone down in the storm.

"No!" he shouted, slamming his hand against the wall.

"What's wrong?" Loretta called from the other room.

With a force of will, he tamped down his rising panic. He'd gotten his message through. They'd find a way to get here in time. Rescue workers were like that. Meanwhile he could call Loretta's doctor on his cell phone.

Taking a deep breath, he went back to the family room.

"What's happening?" she asked. Pain and worry had already etched lines of stress in her face; she looked pinched and scared to death.

Sitting down, he drew his arm around her. "It may take the rescue workers a little longer to get here than we'd hoped."

Her eyes widened. "They're not coming?"

"Sure they are. It's just that with this weather—"

"I can't have this baby alone. I can't do that." Her eyes were wide with panic, her gaze darting around the room as though looking for a way out. "I've never had a baby before. I don't know what to do."

"Shh, sweetheart. Easy does it."

"I promised Isabella." Her voice caught on a sob. "I didn't think I'd have to do it alone. They were going to be with me. I wasn't supposed to be alone.''

"You're not alone, Lori." Never in his wildest imagination had he thought he'd actually have to put into practice what little he'd learned on the Internet about childbirth. He'd only wanted to be *informed*. But now Loretta needed him. He wouldn't fail her— not in the way the doctors had failed his mother. "I'm right here with you. Whatever happens, we'll do this together.''

Chapter Ten

Loretta sagged against him. "I can't do this. It hurts too much."

"You're doing fine. Try to relax and don't fight the pain."

She'd been restless, unable to relax, and they'd been marching around the house for two hours now, since her water had broken. It was past midnight, the rain was still coming down hard, and he was as exhausted as Loretta and even more of a nervous wreck. There was no sign of rescue workers arriving on the scene; the main phone was still out and he was scared to death they'd lose power, too.

"I think I need to sit a minute."

He held her face between his hands. "We're in this together, remember? If you have to rest, we'll do it. Whatever you feel like doing is the *right* thing, you got it?"

Her weary, pain-filled eyes held his. "You must think I'm a terrible wimp."

"You are the strongest, the most courageous woman I've ever met." He placed a heartfelt kiss on her sweat-dampened forehead. "And you're going to have the most beautiful baby in the world. She'll look just like you."

She smiled weakly. "You're good for a woman's ego."

"I aim to please, ma'am."

Wincing as another pain started, she pursed her lips. "How much longer, do you suppose?"

"As long as it takes."

When she managed to rest he brought her a cool cloth for her head and some ice chips to suck. He called the doctor again. And 911. They knew they needed help but no one could get to them. Not for a while. Bulldozers were trying to make a path through the mud slides that had closed the road, but it was a losing battle.

Finally he took her upstairs, where he'd prepared the bed as the doctor had instructed. Water was boiling on the stove. Towels were ready. He'd sterilized a pair of scissors to cut the cord.

God, he was scared.

He eased her down to the bed. "Okay, let's get your clothes off, and we'll start those relaxation exercises. Sure glad I'm a certified Lamaze coach."

She looked at him wildly, a flush returning color to her otherwise pale cheeks. "I can't get undressed in front of you. We're not...I mean—"

"Honey, the way this whole business is going, I'm going to get a lot more intimate with you before the night's over than I've ever been with a woman in my life. I'd say this was no time to turn modest on me."

"You're right. Of course." She turned her back to him while she slipped off her blouse. Her skin was creamy and smooth. Caressable. Her shoulders gracefully sloped, her neck delicately arched.

He'd invited other women to his bedroom for far different reasons, but none had seemed more beautiful, more desirable, and never had he felt more emotional about what they were going to share in the next few hours. The realization that this tiny, stubborn, determined woman would soon give birth to a child brought tears to his eyes.

The realization that she could die nearly crippled him.

"Here, let me help you." He took her blouse, carefully folding it and setting it aside on top of the chest of drawers.

She wrapped her arms around herself as though chilled. "I've got a nightgown..."

"Wear my shirt." Stepping to the closet, he grabbed the first shirt he touched, a hand-tailored blue silk that he'd picked up on a trip to Asia visiting suppliers.

Her fingers clutching the fabric, she looked up in surprise. "I'll ruin this."

"Doesn't matter, sweetheart. Lots more where that came from."

Releasing her bra, she let it slide to the floor, quickly pulling on the shirt before he got more than a glimpse of her full, ripe breasts.

Toeing off her shoes, she removed her slacks, her back still toward him.

"You want to lie down?" he asked. I'll give you a back rub like on the video."

"That'd be wonderful."

She managed to get down on the bed, curling onto her side. "My grandmother gave birth to all her babies at home in her own bed. That's all they had then."

"I hear doing it at home is the latest fad. What goes around comes around, huh?" Two thousand years of progress and she was stuck with Griffin for a midwife.

Another pain gripped her. She moaned softly.

"Think about something beautiful," he urged her as he rubbed his palm over the small of her back. Her stomach might be huge but she wasn't carrying a single ounce of extra fat. She should have been eating better—forget the damn tofu!

She squeezed her eyes closed against the pain. "At church on Mother's Day. There's a stained-glass window. The sun was shining through it that morning. So lovely. A rainbow of colors. For a moment I thought it was my mother sending me a message...." Her breath caught on a pain he didn't think had anything to do with labor. "And then a cloud went by. I knew—"

"You're going to be such a wonderful mom.

Mari's a really lucky kid.'' Bending over, he shifted the dark skein of hair away from her neck and kissed it lightly. ''I bet she's going to be some kind of a pistol.''

''You think so?''

''She's got you for a mom, doesn't she?''

''Isabella—''

''Hey, she's been hanging around with you for the past nine months, hasn't she? I figure she'd absorbed some of your starch. Lord knows what's going to happen after you influence her for eighteen years with your stubborn streak.''

Twisting her head, she grinned up at him. ''One of my most admirable characteristics.''

''You got that right, sweetheart.''

After that they got into a routine. He rubbed. She groaned. He argued with her. When she had the energy, she fought back.

It was the most daring game he'd ever played. And her life was at stake. Griffin wasn't always sure she realized that.

He did.

The pale image of his mother lying in her casket kept haunting him. And his guilt.

''Stay with me, baby,'' he urged as her pains grew more intense. He didn't want to lose her, not his butler. *His Loretta.*

When her moans turned to screams she couldn't control, Griffin said, ''I'd better take a look.''

When the pain eased, she raised her knees. ''I'm so embarrassed.''

He gave her his most wicked smile. "Hey, give me a break. I haven't had a chance to play doctor and nurse with a girl since third grade."

Thank God she laughed at his feeble joke.

He nearly fainted when he saw the baby's head start to crown then disappear. "Not much longer now, sweetheart."

Minutes stretched into another hour as he held her, cajoled her, praised her for all her hard work. She held his hands so tightly, he thought his bones might break. With every contraction, he labored, too. And in between he prayed.

"Grif!"

"Yes, honey, I'm here."

"The baby—" A scream ripped from her throat.

In terror, Griffin switched positions. He got there just in time for a tiny, slick, beet-red little creature to slip into his waiting hands. His eyes glazed with tears. For a minute his fears immobilized him. Blood. Crimson against the stark, white sheets. His mother's skin turning ashen. Her baby so still. Like this child.

"Grif?" Loretta's voice was weak. Fearful.

Griffin jerked back from his paralysis, turned the baby and slapped her bottom.

The baby drew her first breath of air and cried.

A grin stretched Griffin's face. "Oh, baby, you did it," he said, unsure if he was speaking to Loretta or the infant in his hands.

Emotion expanded in his chest, making each beat of his heart a painful tightening that tried to deny him breath. Quickly clamping and cutting the cord, he wrapped the baby in a soft towel, wiping her carefully, every part of her perfect. Her nose, her eyes, a tiny chin. The right number of fingers and toes.

In awe he laid Maria Isabella Santana on her mother's belly, and the baby howled, her lusty lungs venting fully.

"She's beautiful," Loretta whispered. "Isabella would be so happy." Tears edged down her cheeks, and there were deep bruises of fatigue beneath her dark, luminous eyes. Her mussed hair was plastered to her head, yet her smile was angelic.

"Yes." Griffin had never known a sensation as powerful as the one he experienced now. He couldn't name it. Nor did he want to.

They weren't out of the woods yet. If help didn't get here soon, she could bleed to death. He couldn't let that happen.

With limited skill, a little common sense, and a lot of prayer, he helped her deliver the afterbirth, hating her pain, her ashen color frightening him.

Then he changed the sheets, eased into bed and gathered her into his arms.

As he held Loretta and she held her baby, he simply let his feelings wash over him, emotions more powerful than he'd ever experienced before. Later he'd try to analyze them. Much later.

Slowly he became aware that the storm had ceased, the rain dripping from the eaves no more than an occasional drop.

Reaching to the side of the bed, he flicked the switch that drew back the skylight.

A sky pink with the promise of a new day appeared. He brushed a kiss to the top of Loretta's head.

"Pretty romantic, huh?" he whispered.

"Perfect. Thank you." She smiled at him, her eyelids closed, and she slept with her baby in her arms.

With the late-morning sun streaming through the skylight, Loretta couldn't keep her eyes off her baby. What a miraculous sight, the way her bow mouth worked as she slept. Her tiny fingers pulled into fists as though she was ready to take on anyone who objected to her untimely arrival. Her dark eyes, when they opened, explored her unfamiliar world. The doctor had already been—courtesy of the local emergency services team—and pronounced the baby perfect. Only moments ago he'd left the room with Griffin, both of them all smiles.

Loretta rubbed the back of her hand along Mari's downy-soft cheek. The entire ordeal had been something of a miracle, and Griffin had been the miracle worker.

At the moment of Mari's birth, Loretta had not been able to tell whom she loved most—her baby— or the man who had held her through the long night. Her life had been in his capable hands.

And she would never, ever forget the raw rasp of

his voice just before she'd slipped into sleep. "Please don't let her die."

And so now he also held her heart in those same gentle hands.

The change had come on her slowly, she realized. She hadn't loved him at first sight. Certainly not that first night when he'd chased her into the kitchen. Or, at least, she'd thought he was chasing after her, she remembered with a tender smile.

It might have happened when he'd been making pizzas at Marco's shop. That could have been the moment she fell in love. Or perhaps at the picnic when he'd charmed her mother.

But last night she'd realized she could no longer deny the truth.

She loved Griffin Jones.

Surely, among all the foolish things she'd done in her life, that was the most outlandish.

What chance did she have with Griffin, a millionaire playboy whose romantic exploits had been featured on the front pages of the tabloids? As kind as he'd been, as thoughtful and concerned, he could never love her in return. She didn't have enough style, enough class.

Tears threatened again, her emotions on a roller coaster, and she cupped Mari's small head. How Loretta wished she could give her baby a daddy like Griffin, a man who would love her, provide for her and guide her. But that dream wasn't in the cards.

There was a light rap on the door and Griffin peeked inside. "The doc's gone."

"Thank goodness Caltrans was able to make a temporary bridge for you so quickly. I wasn't eager to be airlifted to the hospital in a helicopter."

Grinning, he stepped into the room, eyeing the baby. "Mari's sleeping again?"

Loretta nodded. "A full tummy is a happy tummy."

"The doctor tells me you're in great shape, considering what you've been through, and the baby's fine. No reason for either of you to go to the hospital."

"I had a good Lamaze coach." Unable to help herself, she reached up and took his hand. His fingers were long and tapered, almost artistic, but she knew just how strong they could be, too. And gentle. "Have I told you how much I appreciate all you did for me? For us?" She glanced at the baby sleeping beside her in Griffin's bed. "We'll never be able to thank you enough."

"You did all the work, Lori. I was just along for the ride." Gingerly he sat down beside her. "Doc prescribes rest and plenty of good food so you'll get your strength back. What are you hungry for? Something with lots of antioxidants, I suppose."

She wrinkled her nose. "Right about now, I'd give my left arm for a Big Mac, but I suppose that's too much to ask."

Griffin smiled. "I'll call your family to let them know everything's okay. My guess is I can convince one of 'em to stop somewhere to pick up a burger and fries for you. They're all anxious to see you and the baby.''

At the moment she would be content to simply lie here holding Griffin's hand. But he had work to do. It was only a few days until Christmas. His business needed his attention.

And soon Rodgers would be coming home.

Her heart heavy in her chest, Loretta realized she'd have to leave when he returned. Her temporary job would be over.

By afternoon Griffin realized why hospitals limited the number of visitors a patient could have. He'd been overrun by Santanas who came to ooh and aah over the baby. Forget that they'd arrived with armloads of baby clothes, casseroles and good intentions; they were wearing Loretta out and exposing Mari to God knows what kind of germs.

Warned by thundering footsteps in the hallway, he dodged out of the path of Brian and Cody, who were apparently leading a Power Ranger attack on some hidden enemy. He was definitely going to have to send these people home so Loretta could get some rest.

He started up the stairs, only to be met by Loretta's cousin Brenna coming down them. She was a little older than Loretta, and her figure had begun to thicken.

"The baby's so sweet," she said. "And so much hair. My boys were like that."

In spite of himself, a potent sense of fatherly pride

filled Griffin as though he were responsible for Mari's good looks and sweet disposition. "Yeah, well...look, Loretta needs to get some rest. Can you help me get all these people out of the house?"

"Oh, sure. They know they can't stay long. It's just that everybody feels a little possessive of that baby. She's such a wonderful gift for the family after the tragedy of losing Isabella."

"I understand. But I'd appreciate it if you can move them along a little. I don't want Loretta to get overtired."

"I can certainly sympathize with that," she said with a smile. "And whenever she's ready to move to our place, I've got the porch all set for her."

He frowned, looking up at Brenna, who'd halted a few steps above him. "Porch?"

"It's a glassed-in porch. I offered her the boys' room but she didn't want to put them out. I dyed some old sheets and made curtains for her so she'd have some privacy. Nothing fancy but it'll do fine until she can get a place of her own. The whole family feels as if we need to help out as much as possible since Lori does so much for the rest of us. And my boys will love having her there."

"Isn't a porch going to be too cold for the baby? I mean, it is winter, after all."

She shrugged. "I put a space heater out there, and the room gets lots of sun. It's not like this is Minnesota or anything. She won't freeze. And if it gets too chilly for her, she can certainly come inside. She and the baby will be okay."

Griffin didn't agree. A new mother and baby ought to have better accommodations than something makeshift. After what Loretta had been through, she *deserved* luxury.

With Brenna's help, he herded the Santana clan out of the house, regretting momentarily that Caltrans had been so efficient about building him a temporary bridge. Isolation had a certain appeal at the moment.

So did seeing to it that Loretta had a better place to stay than on Brenna's porch.

Chapter Eleven

"There's no reason for you to move back to your own room so soon," Griffin insisted. He had the baby in one arm, cradling her like a football, and was helping Loretta down the stairs. "I can sleep in the guest room for a night or two."

"No telling how many times Mari will wake up in the night. I don't want her to bother you."

"It wouldn't be a bother," he said grumpily. "I could help take care of her, or something."

She smiled, touched by his concern for both her and her baby. But she didn't dare get used to his caring. He'd already done too much, including fixing meals for her.

"For what she'll be wanting in the night," she said, "I suspect I'm better equipped to handle the problem than you are."

He cocked an eyebrow. "She's a lucky kid."

A flush crept up her neck to heat her cheeks. That afternoon he'd caught her nursing Mari. Although she'd covered up quickly, she'd seen a hungry look in his eyes that had little to do with Mari's beverage of choice—a look that had made Loretta feel extraordinarily feminine. All the more reason why she needed to remove herself from his bed.

They settled Mari into a bassinet that had magically been delivered that afternoon, at no small expense to Griffin, Loretta suspected. And for a while Loretta sat with him in the family room watching a Christmas special on TV, fighting off her fatigue. But soon her eyelids were closing on their own.

Later she thought he must have carried her to bed, though she couldn't quite remember. But she did recall the warm glow of feeling safe in his arms.

The next morning the phone rang while she was in the kitchen fixing herself some tea. Knowing Griffin was already gone, she picked up quickly, afraid the sound would wake Mari.

"Jones residence, the butler speaking."

"Ah, Miss Santana. Your presence continues to surprise me."

"Hi, Rodgers." Her heart stumbled at the sound of his voice. Closing her eyes, she sent up a little prayer that he'd decided to remain in England. Or visit the Caribbean. Anywhere as long as she could be Griffin's butler for a few more precious days. "Yes, I'm here."

"Quite right. Well then, would you pass on the

word to Mr. Jones that I shall be returning home tomorrow evening?''

Tomorrow? That was too soon! She wanted more time. ''Are you sure you can get a flight? Holiday travel—''

''I have my ticket in hand, my dear. No need to worry on my account.''

''Great. I'll be sure to tell Mr. Jones you're coming.''

''Jolly good. I'll just pop off then. I've a date at the theatre, don't you know.''

She wished him a pleasant evening and hung up. From the other room she heard the tiny cries of her baby calling to her. Instantly her breasts responded with a tingling sensation, and she hurried to feed her daughter.

Between frequent nursings, naps and fixing herself some lunch, the day flew by. Suddenly it was dark outside. Griffin hadn't come home early, as he'd hoped.

He was a busy man, Loretta admonished herself. And he'd already done more than enough to help her. There was no need to worry. The delay was probably due to no more than heavy traffic.

But when the doorbell rang, her heart lodged in her throat. What if he'd been in an accident? What if—

Breathlessly, Mari in her arms, she scurried the length of the house and yanked open the front door.

Aileen Roquette narrowed her unnaturally blue

eyes at Loretta. Contacts, she concluded—phony ones.

"I see you're still here." Her gaze flicked over Mari as if she were no more than an object to be dispensed with as unimportant.

Gritting her teeth, Loretta clasped Mari protectively to her chest. Why did everyone expect her to vanish at the snap of their fingers like some kind of a magician's stage trick?

"Good evening, miss," she said in her most butlerlike tone. "I'm afraid Mr. Jones isn't—"

At that precise moment headlights swept across the driveway and Griffin's car pulled up in front of the house. What rotten timing! Loretta could have gotten rid of the redhead easily, if only—

"Hello, darling." Waving, Aileen called to Griffin as he got out of his car. She walked down the steps, her hips rotating in the same rhythm as a cobra sways when it's about to strike.

"Hi, Aileen. This is a surprise."

"Sometimes the mountain has to come to Mohammed."

Loretta thought she was going to throw up.

Pivoting on her heel, she marched back into the house. It was no good. She might be able to dream about being Griffin's long-term butler or even occupying his guest bedroom for a short while.

But there was no way she could compete with Aileen Roquette. It simply wasn't in the cards. And she'd seen how his eyes had lit up at the sight of the stately starlet.

Well, Loretta wasn't going to sit around waiting
to be canned. Rodgers would be back tomorrow.
And Aileen, sexpot that she was, would soon have
her brightly polished fingernails into Griffin—probably occupying the very bed where Loretta had
given birth to Mari.

That image nearly drove Loretta to her knees.

No, rather than endure the very real possibility of
Griffin bringing home a string of beautiful women,
Loretta would leave now. Tonight. As soon as she
could pack her bag and get Mari organized. It was
the only reasonable thing to do.

It was the only thing Loretta could do to protect
herself from needing gallons of tonic to mend a broken heart.

As quickly as he could, and probably none too
graciously, Griffin begged off from taking Aileen to
a Hollywood party that evening. She wasn't likely
to forgive him anytime soon. Not that he cared.

The stricken look on Loretta's face when he got
out of the car had staggered him, and then she'd fled
inside. Something was wrong. He felt it in his gut.

Dear God, the baby!

What if Mari was sick? What if the doctor had
missed something during his all-too-brief examina-
tion?

Griffin cursed himself for not calling a specialist,
for not taking both Loretta and the baby to the hospital, despite what the doctor had said. Women died
in childbirth. *And babies died, too.*

Taking the front steps two at a time, he raced into the house. The guilt that he was somehow responsible for his mother's death and that of his baby sister rose again like a tidal wave. Irrational or not, he couldn't fight the feeling.

"Loretta!" he bellowed, speeding toward the back of the house, to her room. "Where are you?"

She stepped out into the hallway, frowning. "Shh. You'll wake the baby."

He skidded to a halt. "She's okay?"

"Of course she is. Why wouldn't she be?"

"I don't—" He slumped against the wall. God, he was acting like a crazy man—for all the world like a new father. But he wasn't Mari's dad. Or Loretta's husband. He wasn't the sort of man who believed in commitment. Or family. He'd never wanted to be responsible. That's how he'd played it for as long as he could remember—since his mother died.

He looked past Loretta into the bedroom, hoping to get a reassuring glimpse of Mari. What he saw was Loretta's suitcase on the bed, her clothes laid out beside it as though she were packing.

Anxiety crawled along his spine. "What are you doing?"

Her gaze slid away from his. "I'm packing. Mari and I are leaving."

"You can't do that."

"Brenna's all set for us. It's almost Christmas and that's the time when families ought to be together. Brian and Cody are so excited about—"

"You and the baby will be sleeping on a porch, dammit! You'll both freeze."

She whirled, snatched up a blouse, folded it roughly and stuffed it into the suitcase. She'd worry about wrinkles later. Right now she didn't want Griffin to see the tears in her eyes or guess how much she would miss him. "We'll be fine."

"What about me?"

She froze. Her heart slammed against her rib cage, and she swallowed hard. "You?"

"Well, you're my butler, right? What if I need you?"

Disappointment tumbled through her. Even with all that they'd shared—their kisses, the birth of Mari—Loretta should not have expected more. *Used goods* couldn't compete with Hollywood starlets.

"Rodgers will be back tomorrow night. He called." Her vision blurred as she crammed more clothes into the suitcase. "And I'm sure your uncle Matt would be happy to have you to Christmas dinner. Family's important...."

Griffin didn't respond. She didn't know if he was still standing there, or if he'd simply shrugged, agreeing with her decision to leave, and walked away. But she didn't look. She didn't dare let him see the tears tracking down her cheeks.

She hadn't brought much with her, but with the addition of Mari and all the baby paraphernalia it was more than Loretta could carry to the car in one load. Pulling herself together, she zipped the suitcase shut and closed her fingers around the handle.

She turned to discover Griffin standing in the doorway, a curious hint of sadness in his silver-blue eyes. Had he been there all along, silently watching her? Or had he left and returned again?

"Here. I want you to take this." He handed her a check.

"The temporary agency pays me when I turn in my time card. You don't have to—"

"Think of it as a Christmas bonus. For you and the baby."

She glanced at the check, expecting a modest amount, a nominal gift from her employer. Her eyes widened in astonishment. "Griffin, this is too much. I only worked for a month—"

"If you want to live with your cousin for a couple of days, through the holidays, it's okay. Then I want you to use that money to get yourself an apartment. Some place where you and Mari can be comfortable. And warm. And that ought to be enough money to tide you over for a while so you don't have to work right away. You can stay home with the baby. Or even go back to school, if that's what you want."

His generosity stunned her. Not because she was thrilled by his largesse but because she desperately wanted him to give her something that money could never buy. The check represented as much as she could earn in six months. She'd happily tear it up if only he would say the words her heart wanted to hear.

Shaking her head, she handed it back to him. "I can't take your money, Griffin. I've done nothing to earn it.'' She could work her fingers to the bone and it would never be enough to win his love, the only thing she truly wanted.

"It's a gift. I've got more money than I'll ever be able to spend, and now that Compuware and Compuworks are very likely going to merge, the company profits will soar. Take it, Lori. I don't need it.''

"Neither do I,'' she said softly, her heart breaking.

He looked perplexed by her refusal. But she couldn't explain it to him. It would be like explaining a joke to someone who just didn't get it. Love lost all meaning if you had to beg for it. And in some ways she'd been doing that all of her life.

This time she had no chance at all.

Griffin carried her suitcase out to her car and strapped the infant seat securely in the back seat. He didn't understand why she had to leave now; he couldn't figure out why the empty sensation in his chest was so darn painful. Loretta had her own life to lead. Her own family. He didn't need to feel responsible.

"You could wait till tomorrow,'' he suggested lamely. He took Mari from her, holding the baby in his arms, remembering how only yesterday she'd slid brand new and squalling into his hands. "There's no rush for you to leave.''

"I'll be able to help Brenna make pies—''

"You shouldn't be on your feet yet, not long enough to make pies. You just had a baby.'' *His* baby, he almost blurted out, desperate not to let Loretta leave him—desperate not to lose her.

She touched his arm, her eyes luminous in the outdoor lights that flooded the front of the house. "Could you put the baby in her car seat?" Her voice sounded unsteady. "Please. I've really got to go."

"Sure." Awkwardly, because the car was so damn small, he placed Mari in her chair. He brushed a kiss to her forehead and smoothed her cap of dark hair. Her cheeks were so soft; her fingers so tiny and delicate. He'd meant to buy Loretta another car, a bigger, newer one. Something safe—

"Grif?"

Unobtrusively he swiped the tears from his eyes and backed out of the car. By the time he closed the door, Loretta was already behind the wheel. What was her damned hurry?

"Take good care of—" His throat had closed down so tightly, he couldn't finish the thought.

Twisting the key, she cranked over the engine. It sputtered and coughed, dying before it even got started.

Griffin was dying, too.

If she didn't want his money what could he give her to make her stay?

Every woman he'd dated had had her eye on his bank account. He'd never fooled himself about that. But not Loretta. She spent her life giving to others, never taking anything for herself.

She tried the key again. The engine caught, the one bad cylinder clattering and rocking the car.

Her smile strained, she waved. "Take care of yourself." The car lurched forward, the backfire exploding into the cold, night air.

He felt as though he'd been shot. His life blood was draining from him as the car crept steadily down his driveway. Loretta was leaving him. It was like reliving the loss of his mother and the baby sister he hadn't wanted.

But he did want Mari...and Loretta, too, he realized in a panic. He wanted the family they could be, with picnics together and holiday celebrations. More kids. Cousins by the dozens.

Slowly he broke into a jog following the car down the hill. In a panic, his adrenaline flooding his body, the picture of his life came into clear focus for the first time, and realization dawned.

He'd been given a second chance. By letting Loretta go, he'd blown it.

Knowing now what he had to do, he picked up speed. His dress shoes slipped on the asphalt and he went down on one knee. Loretta's car was almost at the bridge. In a minute she'd be gone, maybe forever. Righting himself, he started to run.

"Loretta!"

She didn't hear him; she didn't stop. The damn car engine was too noisy.

Leaving the driveway, he plunged through the bushes to cut her off. He had to catch her—

The car reached the bridge, a narrow span little wider than the car itself, a makeshift affair Caltrans had installed temporarily. The engine backfired again. Black smoke spewed into the air and the old Datsun came to a jerking halt right in the middle of the bridge.

Bless Roberto!

Edging cautiously past the back bumper, he reached the driver's door. "You can't go."

She was frantically twisting the key but having no success getting the car running again. "It'll start. It always does. Eventually."

"No, I mean I won't *let* you go."

She looked up at him, her cheeks wet with tears, and his heart soared. Why hadn't he recognized sooner how much he loved this stubborn, determined woman? This woman who gave so much of herself.

Opening the door, he gently pulled her from the car so he could hold her in his arms. She trembled slightly.

"I can't...stay," she whispered.

"You have to. If you leave me now, my yin and yang will get all messed up, and my electrolytes will go from positive to negative. I probably won't be getting enough vitamin E and I'll get all stressed out. I'll undoubtedly come to a bad end. You don't want to be responsible for that, do you?"

She sniffed, blinking back her tears. "No."

"Without you watching out for me, my enzymes will fall apart and I won't have any resistance left at all. The first germ that passes my way, I'll catch. That'd be terrible."

"Terrible," she echoed. "But I can't—"

"Marry me, Loretta. Let me take care of you for the rest of your life…and have you take care of me."

"But…the baby. She's not even yours."

He framed Loretta's face between his hands, her features already so precious to him he didn't imagine life would be worth living without seeing her every morning…and every night. "I helped bring Mari into this world. In every way that matters she's my daughter as much as she is yours. I love her, Loretta. Almost as much as I love you."

She blinked, disbelieving. "You love me?"

"Desperately, now and forever. Till death do us part."

For a frightening heartbeat, she hesitated. Then a smile banished the tears from her eyes. "Oh, Grif, driving away from you was the hardest thing I've ever had to do in my life. I thought—"

"It doesn't matter what you thought. Just tell me you love me and will marry me. You're the only Christmas present I'll ever want. Say yes, my beautiful butler."

"Yes, I love you. Yes, I'll marry you." She said it with a sigh, the love in her eyes speaking volumes about the happiness she would bring into Griffin's life…and the promise of all the joy the future would bring them and their children. Lots of them.

Epilogue

A mass of red and white poinsettias decorated the chapel, the fragrance of burning candle wax filling the room. The church bells began to chime as the priest pronounced them man and wife.

Feeling as though the past few days had been a dream come true, Loretta could barely contain her joy and excitement. She wasn't at all sure how Griffin had managed to schedule their wedding so quickly, particularly on Christmas Eve. She suspected his long meeting with the priest had resulted in a substantial contribution to the local parish. He'd had another appointment with the head of the marriage license bureau. Who knew how much that had cost him.

She was in awe, too, of her mama's efficiency, burning the midnight oil in order to alter her own wedding dress for Loretta to wear today. She had made it quite clear nothing less than the lace and tulle gown she had been married in would be adequate for her daughter's wedding to such a fine, handsome man as Mr. Jones.

Loretta's family had all come to the service, every one of them willing to give up their own plans for Christmas Eve in order to attend her last-minute wedding. Grif's uncle and aunt were there, too, and Ralph was serving as his best man. She'd chosen Brenna as her matron of honor; Brian and Cody served as dual ring bearers.

In an amazing feat for the holiday season, almost overnight Rodgers had arranged gourmet catering for the reception to take place at Griffin's house. *Their* house, she mentally corrected with secret pleasure and pride.

Looking up expectantly at her groom, Loretta smiled. Though she'd tried to talk him into a spring wedding, he'd insisted he didn't mind delaying the usual intimacies of marriage until she was healed from having her baby.

"You may kiss your bride," the priest said.

Loretta caught the hungry glint in Griffin's eyes as he dipped his head toward hers to seal their marriage vows. His lips were warm and tender, the kiss a promise of more to come, of all he would demand and she would eagerly give. As soon as Loretta was able, she intended to make their delayed honeymoon well worth his time.

The baby squirmed in her arms, demanding her fair share of attention. The priest had thought it a bit unconventional that Loretta carried Mari down the aisle instead of flowers, but Griffin had insisted.

"She's my baby bonus for marrying you," he'd assured her. "Since we're going to be a family together, we might as well start it off right."

Standing on tiptoe, Loretta gave him another quick kiss. "Merry Christmas, Mr. Jones. Welcome to the family."

* * * * *

If you enjoyed what you just read,
then we've got an offer you can't resist!

Take 2 bestselling love stories FREE!

Plus get a FREE surprise gift!

Start celebrating Silhouette's 20th anniversary
with these 4 special titles by
New York Times bestselling authors

Fire and Rain
by Elizabeth Lowell

King of the Castle
by Heather Graham Pozzessere

State Secrets
by Linda Lael Miller

Paint Me Rainbows
by Fern Michaels

On sale in December 1999

Plus, a special free book offer inside each title!

Available at your favorite retail outlet

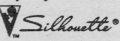

Visit us at www.romance.net

PSNYT

EXTRA! EXTRA!

The book all your favorite authors are raving about is finally here!

The 1999 Harlequin and Silhouette coupon book.

Each page is alive with savings that can't be beat!

Getting this incredible coupon book is as easy as 1, 2, 3.

1. During the months of November and December 1999 buy any 2 Harlequin or Silhouette books.

2. Send us your name, address and 2 proofs of purchase (cash receipt) to the address below.

3. Harlequin will send you a coupon book worth $10.00 off future purchases of Harlequin or Silhouette books in 2000.

Send us 3 cash register receipts as proofs of purchase and we will send you 2 coupon books worth a total saving of $20.00 (limit of 2 coupon books per customer).

Saving money has never been this easy.

Please allow 4-6 weeks for delivery. Offer expires December 31, 1999.

I accept your offer! Please send me (a) coupon booklet(s):

Name: _____

Address: _____ City: _____

State/Prov.: _____ Zip/Postal Code: _____

Send your name and address, along with your cash register receipts as proofs of purchase, to:

In the U.S.: Harlequin Books, P.O. Box 9057, Buffalo, N.Y. 14269
In Canada: Harlequin Books, P.O. Box 622, Fort Erie, Ontario L2A 5X3

Order your books and accept this coupon offer through our web site
http://www.romance.net
Valid in U.S. and Canada only.

PHQ4994R